THE GUNSMITH

441

Aces & Queens

THE GUNSMITH

441

Aces & Queens

J.R. Roberts

SPEAKING VOLUMES, LLC
NAPLES, FLORIDA
2018

Aces & Queens

ISBN 978-1-62815-933-2

Chapter One

Aces and Queens was Clint Adams' favorite poker hand.

With it he had won a big pot, from a table of talented poker players, including Luke Short, two brothers, Bret and Bart, and a fellow named Brady. It had been years ago, but he still remembered the feeling of satisfaction. There wasn't that much money involved, but it was "big" because of who he won it from that night.

The rest of the night those players eventually picked him clean, but that one pot stuck with him forever.

Aces and Queens.

Certainly a better hand than Aces & Eights, the hand his friend Hickok had been holding in Deadwood when he was shot from behind.

But he wasn't thinking of either hand, or even poker, when he came within sight of the town of Kingman, Arizona. He was only thinking of a good steak, a cold beer, and a soft mattress.

***

Clint had been riding for days, most of them in the Mohave, looking for a man named Resnick. He was doing a favor for his friend Talbot Roper, who had made the mistake of taking on two jobs at the same time, Roper was the best private detective in the country, but there was no way he could be in two places at once. So he asked Clint to track down a man named Harry Resnick, while he worked on an entirely different case.

Resnick's trail had led Clint a merry, if some serpentine, chase, which for now looked as if it was leading him to Kingman.

Clint didn't mind that. Even if Resnick wasn't there, he would still get the other 3 things he wanted before continuing the search.

He rode into Kingman.

***

The town, though not a very large one, was far from quiet. Music was out in the streets coming from more than one saloon—which were also offering a lot of light streaming from their windows and doors.

Clint rode up to one of them and dismounted. He decided to have the beer before he went looking for the other 2 things he wanted.

The saloon was called The Gold Rush. He went in, found it filled not only with music, but the sound of chips on a poker table, men laughing and arguing.

He went to the bar, where he had to elbow himself a space.

"Beer," he told the bartender.

"Comin' up."

Clint turned to look around. There were several tables of poker going on, but none of the laughter or arguing seemed to be coming from them. The players seemed fairly serious about what they were doing.

"Here ya go," the bartender said.

"Thanks."

Suddenly, the arguing was starting to drown out the laughing.

"What's all the fighting about?" Clint asked.

"They wanna get into the game," the man next to him said.

"Which table?"

"Not any of these," the man on his other side said. "Them fellers wanna try and get into the tournament across the street, at the Buffalo."

"What tournament?"

"My name's Taft. There's big money across the street," the bartender said. "And big players. You ain't heard about it?"

"I've been on the trail a while," Clint said. "Who's playing?"

"I heard Luke Short's over there," one man said.

"And Bat Masterson," another said.

"Well, whataya know?" Clint said. "A couple of friends of mine."

"You a poker player?" Taft asked.

"I am," Clint said, "and I've played with them. But I'm not the gambler they are. And I didn't know about this tournament because I've been tracking a man."

"Led ya here?" Taft asked.

"That's right."

"What's his name?"

"Resnick," Clint said. "Harry Resnick."

"Don't know 'im," Taft said.

"Who's the sheriff here?" Clint asked.

"Name's Hoskins," Taft said. "Lee Hoskins. Been sheriff a few years. Does a good job. He might know about your man."

"I'll check with him," Clint said, "before I get a hotel. Depending on what he tells me, I might not need one."

"Hotel room's gonna be hard," Taft said. "We got three and they're pretty full."

"Then I might end up sleeping in a barn," Clint said.

"What's yer name, friend?" Taft asked.

"Adams, Clint Adams."

"Hey, yer the—" Taft stopped and looked around. "Guess you don't want who ya are shouted all over the place."

"I'd prefer not."

"Well," Taft said, "I got a spare room upstairs. If ya end up stayin' in town, it's yours."

"I appreciate that," Clint said, putting the empty mug down. "Where's the sheriff's office?"

Chapter Two

He followed Taft's directions, walked Eclipse down the street to the sheriff's office. As Taft guessed, Sheriff Hoskins was there, so he'd be available if there was trouble at the big game.

"Resnick?" Hoskins said, after the introductions. He was standing in front of the gun rack on the wall, which was filled with shotguns and Winchesters. "Don't know 'im. That don't mean he ain't here, though."

Hoskins was in his 50s, had probably been a lawman a few other places before Kingman.

"Have a seat. Coffee?"

"Please."

Clint sat and the sheriff poured 2 cups of coffee, then took his behind his desk.

"Afraid you're not gonna find yourself a room in town tonight," Hoskins said. "Not with that tournament goin' on at the Buffalo."

"I heard about that," Clint said. "Seems some friends of mine are there."

"That right? You play?"

"I have, but I'm not here for that."

"This fella Resnick, he know you're trailin' him?" Hoskins asked.

"I hope not."

"Then if he got to town ahead of you, he probably stopped. Maybe even got the last room in town. I can check with the hotel clerks."

"I'd appreciate that."

"Where are you gonna stay? You wanna bunk in one of my cells?"

"The bartender at the Gold Rush said he had a spare room I could have."

"That's Taft. He's a good man."

"Does he own the saloon, too?"

"He sure does."

"How did the Buffalo get the tournament?"

"Well, that's owned by Big Bill Bartlett," Hoskins said. "He's a big gambler hisself, and he's the one put on the tournament."

"Did he put up the prize money?"

"Part of it, but then he took entry fees," Hoskins said. "There's some big money available."

"I guess so," Clint said. "It would take big money to attract players like Luke Short and Bat Masterson."

"And plenty of others," Hoskins said.

"How long has it been going on?" Clint asked.

"Oh, it started this mornin'," Hoskins said, "and it's supposed to go on for days."

"Any trouble yet?" Clint asked. "Because with that many people in town, you know there will be."

"I expect it," Hoskins said, "but nothin's happened yet."

"I don't envy you," Clint said. "I hope you've got deputies."

"Three of 'em," Hoskins said. "Four, if you'll put on a badge."

"Afraid not," Clint said. "Once I determine Resnick's here, I've got to take him back to Denver. And if he's not here, I have to keep tracking him."

"Well," Hoskins said, "in the mornin' I'll check the hotels for ya. If he's not there, though, he could be sleepin' in a barn somewhere."

Clint stood up.

"At least I'll get a good night's sleep," Clint said. "I know it's kind of late, but can I get a steak anywhere?"

"A few places are stayin', open to feed the poker players late into the night," Hoskins said. "I'd try Wellington's, down the street. Best steak in town."

"I'll do that, then," Clint said, "as soon as I take care of my horse."

"Come and see me tomorrow morning," Hoskins said, "and I should have some information for you."

"Thanks, Sheriff."

Clint left the sheriff's office, walked Eclipse down the street to the livery, where he left him in the care of an appreciative hostler, then made his way—with saddlebags and rifle—to Wellington's for an excellent steak dinner with all the trimmings.

***

After the steak, he returned to the Gold Rush Saloon. Still in full swing and presented himself at the bar to Taft, the bartender/owner.

"Here's a key," Taft said. "Go up the stairs, first room on the right. No number on the door."

"I appreciate this."

Taft beckoned Clint to lean in closer. "After you leave," he whispered, "I'm puttin' a plaque on the door that says, 'The Gunsmith slept here.'"

Clint laughed. "You have my blessings."

Chapter Three

Clint was surprised at how clean and well-appointed the room was, better than most hotels he had been in. Apparently, Taft wanted his guests to be happy.

He could hear voices from downstairs and, occasionally, the sound of chips. It was like a sirens song, calling to him, but he wasn't in Kingman to play poker, he was there to do a job.

He got himself comfortable, hanging his gunbelt on the bedpost, removed his boots, unbuttoned his shirt, and reclined on the bed. He took a book from his saddlebags but was too damn tired to read. He ended closing his eyes and drifting off to sleep . . .

***

He woke to silence.

There was no sound from downstairs. He laid there a few moments, listening intently, finally deciding the saloon must be closed. He was still too tired from all the riding, though, to get up and walk to the door to check, and in moments was asleep, again.

***

The next time he woke, the morning sun was coming in the windows, shafts of it just missing the bed. He sat up, feeling well rested. He couldn't hear anything coming from downstairs, but smelled fresh coffee.

He was using the pitcher and basin Taft had made sure was there when a knock came on the door. He opened it to see a girl of about 25, small and pretty, clutching a robe around her.

"Good-morning," he said.

"Mr. Adams, Taft asked if you wanted to have breakfast downstairs with him."

"Tell him I'd be happy to."

"Twenty minutes?"

"That's perfect. Thank you . . . what's your name?"

"I'm Bonnie."

"Thanks, Bonnie."

"You're welcome."

He closed the door, finished washing, got dressed, strapped on his gun and left the room to go downstairs.

***

The saloon girl, Bonnie, rushed downstairs, still in her robe, over to where Taft was setting up a table.

"He'll be down," she told her boss.

"Thanks, Bonnie. You can go and eat with the girls."

She went to the other side of the room, where 2 other girls in robes were sitting, waiting to eat.

"What's he like, Bonnie?" One of the girls asked her as she sat.

"He's real handsome," Bonnie said. "And he seems really nice. He asked me my name."

"Is he really the Gunsmith?" The girl asking questions was a brunette named Darla.

"That's what the boss said," Bonnie answered. "He told me to go upstairs and ask the Gunsmith if he wanted breakfast."

"Shhh," a blonde named Lily hissed, "here he comes!"

***

As Clint came down the stairs he saw 3 girls in robes seated across the room. Taft seemed to have done very well for himself, having hired a blonde, a brunette, and a redhead.

He walked over to where Taft was sitting at a table with a coffee pot in front of him.

"I hope you like your coffee strong," the bartender said.

"That's exactly how I like it."

Taft poured Clint a cup and handed it to him.

"We've got bacon and eggs comin', if that's okay."

"Perfect. If you have a kitchen here, do you serve food?"

"No," Taft said, "we only use it in the mornin' so we can all have breakfast together."

"That makes you a pretty nice boss."

"I try to treat my people good," Taft admitted. "You met Bonnie already, you can meet the other girls later."

"How long did the action go on down here last night?" Clint asked. "I woke up once during the night and didn't hear a sound."

"That must've been around four, when we closed down," Taft said. "I'll be opening the doors again at noon."

A man came from the kitchen, a large white apron spread over an expanse of belly. He carried some plates in his hands and up his arms, walked across the room and served the 3 ladies.

"Ladies first," Clint said, as the man went back to the kitchen. "I see what you mean about treating them well."

The man came out with two more plates, set them in front of Clint and Taft. Clint could see he was in his 50s, with a hairy chest peeking out front beneath the apron, as well as hairy forearms.

"Thanks, Mike."

"Sure, Boss."

He returned to the kitchen.

"You talk to the sheriff last night?" Taft asked.

"I did," Clint said. "He couldn't help me with Resnick, but he's going to check the hotels today to see if he checked in last night."

"What's this guy done?"

Clint wasn't really free to talk about Talbot Roper's case, so he said, "A friend of mine was hired to find him, and I'm helping him out."

"So it's not like a bounty, or anythin'."

"No," Clint said, "nothing like that."

"You're not lookin' to put some lead in him?"

"No," Clint said, "I'm just trying to find him and take him back to Denver."

"And if he don't wanna go?"

"I won't give him a choice."

"Well," Taft said, "if you give me an idea what he looks like, I can keep an eye out for ya."

"He's tall, in his forties, and you can't miss him because he's got a nose like a potato."

"I'll tell the girls to keep a lookout for this potato-nose guy."

As they continued to eat, Clint found out that, as had happened many times before, The Gold Rush had changed hands during a card game.

"Why aren't you playing in the poker tournament?" Clint asked.

"Well, first, I gave the game up after I won this place," Taft said, "Second, the game is across the street, and that's my competition. I'll never set foot in the Buffalo."

"I see."

"But by all means," Taft added, "go across and have a look. After all, your friends are playin' there, right?"

"That's right," Clint said. "When does it start up each day?"

"They'll get it goin' early," Taft said. "Probably started about an hour ago."

"I guess I should go and have a look, then," Clint said. "Who knows, Resnick might be over there." He stood up. "Thanks for breakfast."

He put his hat on and headed for the front door.

"Don't forget," Taft said, "we open at noon."

"I'll remember," Clint said.

As Clint went out Taft shouted, "Bonnie, lock the front doors."

She jumped up from her chair, said, "Right boss," and hurried across the room.

Chapter Four

Clint decided to give the sheriff some time that morning to visit the hotels, so he crossed the street to the Buffalo Saloon and Gambling Emporium. There were two uniformed guards on the front door.

"You a player?" one of them asked.

"No, I'm not."

"Only players can go in," the other man said.

They were both big, burly men, the kind you wanted to hire to guard a game like that. Both were armed with pistols on their hips.

"What if I wanted to be a player?" he asked.

"You'd have to go to the hotel," burley number 1 said.

"Which one?"

They looked at each other, then one said to him, "The Buffalo Hotel," as if it was obvious.

"Right. That where the players are staying?"

"A lot of 'em," burly number 2 said. "The big names."

Clint took a look over the batwing doors, but there was a divider inside, hiding the floor from the outside.

"Where's the Buffalo? Near here?"

"A few blocks that way," burly number 1 said, pointing.

"Thanks."

Clint started walking in the opposite direction of the sheriff's office, a direction he hadn't walked, yet.

When he came to the Buffalo Hotel he was impressed. It looked new, and he had no doubt it was owned by the same person who owned the Saloon, by a man calling himself Big Bill Bartlett.

There were no guards to stop him from entering the hotel, but there was one standing in the lobby. He gave Clint a look, but didn't move from his appointed spot.

Clint went to the front desk.

"I'm sorry, sir, but we're full up," the middle-aged clerk with a mustache said. "There's a poker—"

"I know all about it," Clint said. "Can you tell me if Bat Masterson and Luke Short are in their rooms?"

"No, sir," the clerk said, "they're both in the diningroom, sittin' together."

"Thanks."

"Uh, sir, is there gonna be trouble?" the man asked, nervously.

"Not likely," Clint said. "They're friends of mine."

He turned and headed for the diningroom.

Chapter Five

As he entered the diningroom, he immediately spotted his 2 friends' table. It was in the back, where they both had a good view of the room. As he started for them they saw him and smiled. They both stood and shook hands enthusiastically.

"Clint, you old warhorse," Bat said, "whatayou doin' here?"

"You're not here for the poker game, are you?" Luke asked.

"Nope," Clint said. "I'm doing Tal Roper a favor, trailing a fugitive."

"Sit down, then," Luke Short said. "We got plenty of coffee."

Clint sat with them, but angled his chair so he could also see the entire room.

"I heard about the tournament when I rode in, so I wasn't surprised to hear that you two were here."

"There's big money here," Bat said. "Some of the big boys have turned out."

"And been knocked off," Luke Short said.

"Yeah, Gentleman John Peel got sent home early," Bat Masterson said.

"That's what happens when you sit at my table," Luke said.

"And Brady was at Bat's table," Luke said. He jerked his thumb. "Gone."

"Sounds pretty cutthroat," Clint said.

Bat and Luke kept eating as they talked.

"I sort of expected to see you here," Bat said, "but at one of the tables."

"When Roper got ahold of me and asked for my help, I couldn't say no. So I wasn't around to hear about this."

"There's still time," Bat said. "They're having qualifying games across the street in the Gold Rush. If you win there, you get to move to a main table in the Buffalo."

"I don't have time," Clint said. "I'm still looking for Roper's man."

"Good," Luke said. "I don't want you in this thing, anyway. It's bad enough I'm gonna have to deal with Bat."

"I love you, too, Mr. Short," Bat said, with a smile.

"We have to get goin'," Luke said. "The games have started already."

"Yeah," Bat said, "we're a little late."

"By design, if I know you two," Clint said. "I've got one question before you go."

"What is it?" Bat asked.

"Have either of you heard of a man named Resnick?"

"No," Luke said.

"Doesn't ring any bells with me, either," Bat said.

The 3 of them got up and walked outside together.

"You want to come over and watch?" Bat asked.

"A couple of fellas over there said only players can get in."

Luke said, "We can get you in."

"That's okay," Clint said. "I've got work to do."

"If you change your mind," Bat said, "just tell those two at the door your friends with me and Luke. They'll let you in."

"I'll do that."

Bat and Luke crossed the street and started walking toward the Gold Rush. Clint headed for the sheriff's office.

***

"Come on in," Sheriff Hoskins said. "Pour yourself a cup of coffee."

Clint did as the sheriff invited, then sat across from the man.

"I checked the hotels in town," Hoskins said. "They're all filled up. Your man ain't there."

"Maybe he was looking for a room and they turned him away."

"Nah, nine of them said that," Hoskins answered. "I guess your man knew the town was filled up. He coulda bedded down somewhere and left early. You leave now he's probably not that far ahead of you."

"Which direction?" Clint asked, wondering why the sheriff was in such a hurry to get him gone?

"I thought you were trackin' him," Hoskins said. "Can't you just . . . pick up his trail?"

"I was tracking him, but I'm not an expert," Clint said. "I'll need to have some idea of which way he went when he left town."

"Ah, well . . . I suppose you could ask around, maybe find out where he did bed down. Check the livery stable."

"Is there a rooming house in town?"

Hoskins snapped his fingers.

"I didn't check there," he said.

"And whorehouses?"

Hoskins held up his fingers. "Two."

"Well . . . just tell me where they are and I'll check them," Clint said.

"Sure," Hoskins said. "And maybe durin' my rounds I can find out somethin'."

Clint put the empty coffee cup on the sheriff's desk and stood up.

"I appreciate your help," he said, and left.

Chapter Six

Kingman was busy, but most of the hub-bub was connected to the poker tournament. It had brought many players to town, and they all had to eat, and sleep, buy goods in the stores. And Clint was sure that, with all gambling events—poker, boxing, horse racing—the con men, fast women and pickpockets were also there.

For a moment, as he exited the sheriff's office, he saw a flash of reddish hair across the street, and thought he saw somebody he knew, but just as quickly, she was gone. It might have been his imagination. He hadn't seen that person in many years.

He decided to check the rooming houses first, but they had never heard of nor seen anyone like Harry Resnick. If he was, indeed, in Kingman, did he know somebody who was housing him? Was he here because of the tournament? Or had he already come and gone?

It took most of the morning to check the livery stables and the rooming houses. He tried a couple of whorehouses, but they weren't opening their doors this early in the day, no matter how hard he knocked on their doors.

He decided, since it was after 12 noon, to go over to the Gold Rush Saloon for an early beer.

He was crossing the street to the saloon when he spotted the red hair again. This time he knew it was her and changed his direction.

"Anne!" he called, coming up behind her.

She turned, looked at him and smiled.

"Good God," he said. "I didn't recognize you without your gun, but you're as beautiful as ever."

"Clint Adams!" Anne Archer said. "What a surprise. When was the last time . . ."

"It's been years," Clint said. "Too many."

"Well," she said, "we both have our lives to live, right?"

"I suppose we have."

"What are you doing here in Kingman?"

"Trailing a man."

"You're not huntin' bounty now, are you?" she asked.

"No, that's always been your job, Anne," he said. "Although, I can't imagine you doing it without your gun. And in a dress."

"I know you haven't seen me in a dress very often," she said.

"What's the occasion?"

She looked around, then back at him. She was a little older, but then so was he. There was a time when he thought he might be in love with her. Seeing her now, the feelings were coming back.

"Can we go someplace and catch up?" she asked. "I do have a lot of things to tell. And now that I see you, I've got somethin' to ask."

"I passed a café a couple of blocks back," Clint said. "We could go there and get some coffee."

"Yes, all right," she said.

They walked back to the café, giving him time to take her in. She had always been a lovely woman, but since she worked as a bounty hunter, she always wore men's trail clothes. Now here she was in a simple dress, with her hair down instead of tucked up under a hat, and she was more beautiful than ever.

When they got to the café it was only about half full, and they were able to get a table against the back wall.

"Just two coffees?" Clint told the waiter.

"Yes, sir."

"You haven't told me why you're trailin' this man if you're not huntin' bounty," Anne said.

"As a favor," he said. "You remember me talking about Talbot Roper?"

"Yes, I do," she said. "Your detective friend from Denver."

"That's right," Clint said. "He asked me to track this fella down and bring him back to Denver."

"What's he done?"

"Broke about half a dozen laws, but Roper was hired to bring him back. Apparently, it's a private matter, so I didn't need to know the details."

"You're huntin' a man and you don't know what he's done?" she asked.

"Like I said," Clint said. "It's a favor."

She shook her head and smiled.

"You were always doin' favors for friends and gettin' yourself into trouble for it."

"You should know," Clint said. "I did a few favors for you and your partners. How are Sandy and Littlefeather?" When they met, Anne was riding with her partners Sandy Spillane and Katy Littlefeather, hunting bounty together. They were real good at it.

"We split up," she said. "I don't know what Little-feather's doin' now. I think Sandy's wearin' a badge, somewhere."

"So that brings us to you," Clint said, "and why you're in Kingman wearing a dress and not carrying a gun."

"Well . . ." She looked away for a second, then seemed to steel herself and looked back. "Clint . . . I got married."

Chapter Seven

Clint was shocked.

There had been a time when he thought he and Anne Archer might get married. That was before he realized marriage just wasn't for him. Why, then, did this news hit him so hard?

"Married?"

She nodded.

"When?"

"As it happens, just a few weeks ago."

A coincidence, then, that he would run into her so soon after her wedding.

"Do you live here? You and your husband?"

"No," she said, "we're here . . . he's here for the tour-nament."

"You married a gambler?"

"I didn't know he gambled when I married him," she said. "It all happened kind of fast."

"When did you find out?"

"A few days ago, when he told me we were comin' here, and why."

"So it was a shock?"

"Well, let's say a surprise."

"A terrible surprise?"

"I didn't think so," she said, "but now . . . I don't know."

"Do you want him to stop?" Clint asked.

"I don't know that, either," she said. "I'm not sure how much this means to him. But since we got here, and since it all started, he's been different."

"And?"

"And now I'm wonderin' how different?" she said, playing with her cup, which she hadn't drunk from yet. She was just twirling it. "I mean, is he even the man I thought I married? Today, I was just wanderin' the street, wonderin'—and then I saw you."

That's funny," he said. "I thought I saw you. In fact, I thought I saw you earlier this morning."

"You did," she said, "but I saw you, and I . . . ran."

"Ran? Why?"

She sat back, took her hands away from the cup.

"I saw you across the street and . . . old feelings popped up," she said. "I ran because I didn't need the extra complications. I was already worried about my marriage, which is only weeks old."

"And what's changed?"

"You found me," she said. "And I realized . . . I thought maybe I could . . . ask a favor."

Clint stared at her.

27

"Believe me," she said, "I know how . . . ironic that sounds after our talk about favors, but . . ."

"I'm in the middle of something, Anne," he said, "but . . . tell me what you want, and I'll see what I can do."

"Just like that?" she asked.

He nodded.

"Just like that."

"But . . . why?"

"Let's just say you're not the only one experiencing . . . old feelings."

She picked up her cup and sipped from it.

***

They decided to have something to eat, if only to give themselves time to deal with what had just come up. Clint ordered a bowl of beef stew, while Anne settled for some eggs.

"All right," he said, when they were eating, "tell me about this favor."

She chewed and swallowed before answering.

"I'd like you to find out about my husband," she said.

"Find out what, exactly?"

"Everything," Anne said. "Who he really is, how much the gamblin' means to him."

"Am I going to be surprised when I hear his name?" Clint asked. "You didn't marry someone I know, did you?"

"No," she said, "you don't know him. That's why you're the perfect person to find out who he is."

He put his spoon down and stared across the table at her.

"I don't understand," he said. "You're a smart woman. How did you end up marrying a man you don't really know?"

"I could say I was swept off my feet," she said, "blinded by love, but that makes me sound like a silly woman, not a smart one. Let me just say . . . I thought I knew what I was doing, but apparently I didn't."

"And now you want my help."

"Yes."

"And if I wasn't here?" Clint asked. "If I hadn't seen you, and approached you, what would you be doing now?"

"I suppose," she said, "I wouldn't be wonderin' if we should take this meetin' to your hotel room."

"Anne . . . you're married."

"I'm painfully aware of that right now, Clint. Painfully aware. But you're right." she said, looking at him across the table. "I'm married. It wouldn't be right."

"You love your husband."

"I thought I did," she said. "Now I'm not so sure."

"That's still no reason to—"

"No," she said, cutting him off, "it isn't."

"Is he playing in the main tournament, in the Buffalo Saloon?" Clint asked.

"Yes," she said, "he paid the full thousand-dollar entry fee."

"A thousand?" Bat and Luke hadn't told him that.

"I know," she said. "That's a lot of money. That's when I first got . . . anxious."

Clint could have afforded the fee, but he wasn't sure he would have wanted to. Bat and Luke were such good poker players, and there were others almost as good. Clint felt he was, at best, a talented amateur. Doc Holliday had once told him he could play poker for a living if he put his mind to it.

"I've just been told I can get into the Buffalo to watch the games if I want," Clint said, "so I guess I could just happen to meet your husband."

"I'd really appreciate it, Clint."

"Once I meet him I'll sound him out and see how bad a gambler he really is," Clint added. "Okay, so what's your bridegroom's name?"

"His name's Abel Terrell," she said.

"I never heard of him," Clint said. "I'll check with Bat Masterson and Luke Short to see if they have. If he's a poker player, they'll know."

They finished their meal, Clint paid the check and they stepped outside.

"So where's your gun?" Clint asked.

"What?"

"When you put on the dress what happened to your gun?"

"I still have it," she said. "Abel doesn't like me to carry it, though."

"Does he know what you used to do for a living?"

"He does."

"How did he find that out?"

She looked sheepish, then said, "It's how we met."

"How so?"

"I brought him in for a bounty."

Chapter Eight

Clint went over to the Buffalo.

Now he had taken on a second favor, one for Tal Roper and one for Anne Archer. He figured if anyone in town had seen Harry Resnick, it would be a bartender. Taft hadn't seen him, so at least he could ask the barman at the Buffalo the same question, and maybe do the favor for Anne at the same time.

The same two guards were on the front door when he got there.

"We told you—"

"Bat Masterson told me to come over and have a look," Clint said. "You want to go in and ask him?"

They looked at each other.

"And bother him while he's playing?" he added.

"Ah, what the hell—" burly 1 said.

"Go ahead," burly 2 said. "Let somebody inside toss him out."

"Thanks," Clint said. He slipped between them and went through the doors and around the partition.

It was a big saloon with a long bar, a stage, and the floor was packed with tables of poker players. The sound of chips hitting the table and shuffling cards was almost deafening.

There weren't many customers at the bar, since most everybody was there to play. As he approached, a man tossed down a shot of whiskey, then went back to his table.

"Not a good idea to drink while you play poker," Clint said, to the bartender.

"Tell me about it," the big man said. "How do you think I got to be a bartender? What'll ya have?"

"Beer."

"You playin'?"

"No."

"Then you'll hafta pay for your drinks."

"I always do," Clint said.

The bartender put a mug of beer in front of him.

Clint turned his back to the bar to watch the action. Cards going around and around, chips hitting the table, cards being tossed down, then shuffled and dealt, again. There were girls working the floor for players who wanted to drink at their tables. Clint knew most of those types of players weren't going to do very well.

He spotted the table Bat was sitting at, and another where Luke Short was playing. Bat spotted him, and Clint jerked his chin just enough to get Bat to take a break and come to the bar.

"Beer, please," Bat said.

"Yessir."

Bat looked at Clint.

"Bat, do you know a fella named Abel Terrell?"

"I do," Bat said. "He's sittin' at the table next to mine."

"Did you know him before this?"

Bat shook his head, accepted his beer from the bartender.

"Thanks." He sipped it, then put it down. "No, I didn't know him before. I heard his name because of where his table is. Also, he's been winnin'. I pay attention to the ones who are winnin' at each table."

"Bat, I need to meet him."

"So, introduce yourself."

"I don't want to be obvious about it."

"Well, I could introduce you, but like I said, I don't really know 'im, just enough to point him out."

"Well okay," Clint said, "let's start with that."

"I'll do it on my way back to my table."

"Don't be obvious about it, though."

"Right," Bat said.

He headed back to his table, and as he passed the table to his right he paused just long enough for Clint to see the player he was indicating. Clint nodded, and Bat went back to his table.

Clint figured he'd watch Abel Terrell play for the rest of the afternoon, while talking to the bartender.

"How about another beer?" he asked the man.

"Comin' up."

Chapter Nine

The bartender's name was Eddie Sengler, and he claimed to know almost everybody in town—everyone who ever had a drink in the Buffalo, that is.

"Resnick?" Eddie said. "I don't know 'im. Is he supposed to be livin' here?"

"No, probably passing through," Clint said.

"When?"

"Yesterday."

"Then he couldn't have got in here for a drink," Eddie said. "You got in 'cause you got friends."

"I don't know," Clint said. "Maybe he has friends, too. Maybe that's why he's here."

Eddie shrugged and said, "Maybe."

"Has anybody been around the last couple of days asking for your boss?"

"Mr. Bartlett? There's always people askin' for him."

"Why?"

"Jobs, loans, all sorts of reasons."

"Does he give out loans?"

"To his friends, yeah."

"Well," Clint said, "I guess the only way to find out if Harry Resnick was his friend is to ask him. Where is he?"

"He's in his office, but he don't like to be bothered when he's in there."

"I'm not going to bother him," Clint said, "I'm just going to ask him a few questions."

Clint put his glass down, but Eddie reached out and placed his hand on Clint's arm.

"Ya can't go back there by yourself," he said. "I'll get fired."

"I don't want that to happen," Clint said. "Can you get somebody to take me back, make an introduction?"

"Why don't you have Masterson do it?" Eddie asked. "Big Bill knows him."

"Is Big Bill going to know who I am?"

"Well, sure," Eddie said, "everybody knows the Gunsmith."

"I don't want to get Bat involved," Clint said, "or take him away from his game, again. Let's just have somebody else take me back there. You?"

"I can't leave the bar," Eddie said. "I'll have one of the girls do it."

"That suits me."

Eddie looked around, got one of the girls' attention, and waved her over.

A blonde came walking over, gave Clint a look up and down.

"Yeah, Eddie?"

"Joi," he said, "take Mr. Adams here back to see Mr. Bartlett. And make the introductions."

"Well, Eddie," she said, "first you're gonna have to introduce me."

"Oh, yeah," he said. "Joi Leslie, meet Clint Adams."

"The Gunsmith," Joi said, putting out her hand. "It's a pleasure."

She was a full-bodied blonde with a firm handshake. Clint would have been very interested if he hadn't just spent time with Anne Archer.

"Hello," was all he said.

"This way, please, Mr. Adams," she said, and led the way.

They crossed the floor, darting between tables. He noticed that Joi touched several men on the shoulder along the way—interestingly enough, including Abel Terrell.

When they reached a door against the back wall she knocked and opened it a crack.

"Boss? Fella here wants to meet you."

"Who is it?" a deep voice rumbled from inside.

"His name's Clint Adams?"

"The Gunsmith?" he called out. "Well, don't leave 'im standin' out there, darlin', bring him in."

Chapter Ten

Clint's first look at "Big" Bill Bartlett was a shock.

The man got up from behind his desk, came charging around with his hand out. He was barely 5 ½ feet tall.

"This is a real honor, Mr. Adams," he said, pumping Clint's hand. "What brings you to my humble establishment? Are you looking to get into the game?"

"I'm afraid I don't have time for that, Mr. Bartlett," Clint said.

"Please," Bartlett said, "just call me Big Bill." He looked past Clint. "That's all, Joi. We don't need a chaperone."

"Of course, Big Bill." She backed out the door and closed it behind her.

"Can I offer you a drink?"

"No, thanks . . . Big Bill, I'm fine."

"Then have a seat and tell me what brings you here."

Big Bill went back around his desk and sat. The size of it, and his chair, made him seem even smaller. Clint sat across from him.

"I'm tracking a man and his trail led me here," Clint said. "I wasn't even aware this tournament was going on. I've been on the trail for some time."

"That's too bad," Bartlett said. "We've got some big names in the game, but I would've loved to have you, too."

"Yes, I saw Bat Masterson and Luke Short out there."

"Ah," Bartlett said, his eyes lighting up, "our marquee names, indeed."

"And friends of mine," Clint said. "I'd just as soon not play against them. But my business keeps me from having to make that decision."

"And what is your business?"

"As I started to say, I tracked a man here and I'm wondering if he was just passing through, or if this was his destination."

"What's his name?"

"Harry Resnick."

Bartlett thought it over a moment.

"Resnick, Resnick . . . nope, can't say as I know of anybody living in town by that name."

"Or visiting?"

"If he's visiting, it's not with me," Bartlett said. "What's his business?"

"Conning people," Clint said. "A private detective friend of mine has been hired to take him back to Denver and asked me to help out."

"Well," Bartlett said, "this kind of event we're having here certainly would bring in those kinds of people—con men, shysters, pickpockets and the like. Does he know you're on his trail?"

"That's a good question."

"If he doesn't," Bartlett pointed out, "then you could be right about this being his destination. He might be here to ply his trade. Have you talked to the sheriff?"

"I have," Clint said. "He doesn't know him but is going to be on the look-out."

"What's this fellow Resnick look like?"

"You can't miss him," Clint said. "He's got a nose as big as a potato."

"Certainly sounds like he'd stand out," Bartlett said. "I'll have my security team keep their eyes open."

If he was talking about those two on the front door, Clint didn't hold out much hope for assistance.

"I assume you got past my guards by invoking Bat's name?" Bartlett said.

"It helped."

"Well, you're welcome to stay, or come and go as you wish," Bartlett said.

"I appreciate that, Big Bill."

Both men stood and shook hands over the desk.

"And if you should decide you want to get into the tournament, just let me know. I can keep you from having to play in one of the qualifying games. I'll just put you right at a table."

"Much obliged, Big Bill," Clint said. "I'll keep that in mind."

"You know what? Let me walk out with you. I haven't been on the floor for some hours."

Bartlett came around the desk and walked with Clint to the door. Clint was once again struck by the man's diminutive size. He wondered if the name "Big Bill" was ironic, or if it actually meant something to the man.

Out on the floor they walked between the tables back to the bar.

"I assume you two have met," he said to the bartender.

"We have, sir," Eddie said.

"Well, Mr. Adams is welcome here any time," Bartlett said. "Give him whatever he wants, as if he was one of the players. It's on me."

"Yessir."

"Thank you, Big Bill," Clint said. "I'm sure I'll be back here again."

"Good luck with your search," Bartlett said. "I hope you find him."

Clint left the Buffalo.

Chapter Eleven

There was plenty of the day left, and Clint intended to check the whorehouses as soon as they opened for business.

He didn't go looking for Anne Archer, who had told him she and her husband had a room in the Orchard Hotel. But he had only seen her husband, didn't have anything else to report to her. So he decided to use the rest of the afternoon looking for Harry Resnick.

***

Clint's meal with Anne Archer had been a pretty early lunch, and he started getting hungry for supper around 4. At that time, there was plenty of room in all the restaurants and cafes. He picked out a small place and had a completely edible-yet-forgettable steak.

After that it was time to hit the whorehouses. Since he had already knocked on their doors in vain, he knew where they all were.

At the first one the door opened quickly, this time, A pretty girl in a filmy nightgown told him she had never seen a man with a nose like that.

"Okay, thanks," he said.

"But . . . don't you wanna come in?" she asked.

"No thanks," he said. "Not today."

She opened her gown to show her hard, brown nipples and asked, "Are you sure?"

"No," he said, "I'm not sure," and walked away.

***

At the second whorehouse the door was answered by a tall, broad-shoulder black man.

"Yeah?"

"I'm looking for a fella named Resnick," Clint said. "Would he be a customer here?"

"Don't know nobody by that name," the man said.

"Are you sure?" Clint asked. "Tall, middle-aged man with a huge nose, like a potato."

The big black man frowned and said, "I ain't seen nobody with a nose like that, Mister. You wantin' ta come in here for a poke, or not?"

"Not," Clint said, and before he could do or say anything else, the man stepped back and slammed the door in his face.

Clint turned and walked away, wondering why Resnick had come to Kingman, and where the hell he was? Men stopped in a town for one of several reasons. If they didn't live there they wanted a bed, a steak, a beer, or a poke. Harry Resnick apparently did not want any of those things.

So what did he want?

And did he know he was being trailed?

***

As it got dark Clint decided to turn his attention to Anne Archer's problem. He went back to the Buffalo Saloon and this time the two burly guards made no move to stop him from going in.

"Beer?" Eddie asked, as Clint reached the bar.

"Yeah."

Clint looked around, saw some empty chairs that had been taken earlier.

"Looks like a few players bowed out," he said to Eddie, as he accepted his beer.

"More than a few," Eddie said. "As they lose they bring in players from them games across the street."

"How long is this supposed to go on?" Clint asked.

"Until it's over," Eddie said, "and somebody wins."

Clint looked over at Bat's table, Luke's table, knowing his two friends would still be there, and they were. Then he shifted his eyes to Abel Terrell's table, and Anne's husband was still there, too.

"Eddie, do you know many of these players?" Clint asked.

"Naw," Eddie said. "I mean, I know who Bat Masterson and Luke Short are, Gentleman John Peel when he was here and that gambler Brady, maybe a few more. But I don't know them personal-like."

"See that tall fella at the table next to Bat's. His back's to us, but I think his name's Abel Terrell."

"I see 'im."

"Know anything about him?"

"No."

"How many times does he take a break for a drink?"

"I ain't seen him take a drink, not yet," Eddie said.

"Hmm . . . looks like he's got a pretty good pile of chips in front of him."

"Yeah, must be winnin'."

"Yeah," Clint said, "he must be."

"That makes him a good player, don't it?" Eddie asked.

"Makes him a lucky player," Clint said. "Remains to be seen if he keeps winning. If he does, then that would make him a good player."

"You interested in him?" Eddie asked.

"Just curious, Eddie," Clint said, "just curious."

Chapter Twelve

Clint was still standing at the bar when Luke short came walking over.

"Let me have half a beer, Eddie."

"Yes, sir, Mr. Short."

Eddie filled a mug halfway and set it down in front of Luke Short.

"Any luck with your business, Clint?" he asked.

"Resnick?" Clint shook his head. "No sign of him."

"Then what are ya doin' here?" Luke asked.

"I managed to get myself roped into doing another favor," Clint said. "Do you know a player named Abel Terrell?"

"Not before we got here," Luke said. "He's at a table next to Bat's. Looks to be doin' pretty good, too."

"Lucky or good?" Clint asked.

"I won't know that until I sit at the same table with him," Luke said. He finished his half a beer and set the mug down on the bar. "I've gotta get back to the game. I'm ridin' a hot streak."

"Aren't you always?" Clint asked.

Luke laughed, slapped Clint on the back, and went back to his table.

Clint was about to leave when he looked over at Abel Terrell's table and saw Terrell looking toward the bar. He didn't know if the man was looking at him, or looking for a drink. He waved at Joi to join him at the bar.

"What do you need, Mr. Adams?" Joi asked. "Big Bill says you get whatever you want."

"Do you know who Bat Masterson is?"

"Of course."

"Do you know a man named Abel Terrell?"

"No."

"Earlier, when you walked past his table, you put your hand on his shoulder."

"I did?" she asked. "I do that to a lot of the players."

"What about that tall fella at the table next to Bat's?" Clint said. "His back is to us . . . okay, now he's looking over here." Terrell quickly turned back to his game.

"I don't know him," she said.

"Why don't you go over and ask him if he wants a drink?" Clint said.

Joi shrugged and said, "Okay."

"But ask everybody at the table, so he's not conspicuous."

She strolled over to the table, stopped and asked each player if they wanted a drink, then came back to the bar.

"Three whiskeys, Eddie," she said.

"Is one for him?" Clint asked.

"No," she said, "he didn't want anythin'."

She took the tray of drinks Eddie gave her and carried it over to the table.

Clint looked at Eddie.

"Then why was he looking over here?"

Eddie shrugged.

"Maybe he was lookin' at you," the bartender said. "Word's gone around about who you are."

"Ah," Clint said, "that might explain it."

Suddenly, after Joi had delivered the drinks, Terrell stood up and walked to the bar. He kept a good distance between himself and Clint.

"Can I get a cup of coffee, please?" he asked Eddie.

"Sure thing."

While he waited for Eddie to pour his coffee, Terrell looked over at Clint. He was a tall, handsome man in his 40s, wearing an expensive grey suit.

"So you're Clint Adams?" he asked. "The Gun-smith?"

"That's right."

Terrell accepted his coffee from the bartender, left it sitting on the bar in front of him.

"What brings you to Kingman?" Terrell asked. "It looks like you're not in this tournament."

"You're right, I'm not," Clint said. "And what's your name?"

"Oh, that's right," Terrell said. "You don't know me. My name's Abel Terrell. I'm the man who's going to win this tournament."

"That's an interesting statement," Clint said, "considering you've got the likes of Bat Masterson and Luke Short to deal with."

"They're not going to take this from me," Terrell said. "This is my time."

"Well, in that case, I wish you luck."

"I'm not going to need luck," Terrell said. "I've got the skill, and the cards are running my way."

"And why are you telling me all this?" Clint asked.

"Because I know who you are," he said. "I've heard all about you from my wife, and I'm tired of hearing it. So this week I'm going to make my name."

"Your wife?" Clint asked. He didn't want to admit that he had seen Anne Archer in town, let alone spoken to her. It would probably get her in trouble with her husband. "Who's your wife?"

"Never mind," Terrell said. "I've got a game to get back to. Just remember what I said, Gunsmith. My . . . wife."

Terrell turned, left his coffee on the bar and went back to his table.

Chapter Thirteen

"He what?" Anne Archer asked, a little while later.

"He practically warned me away from you," Clint said.

He had gone to Anne's hotel and when she opened the door he stayed in the hall and told her what had happened.

"He told you we were married?"

"Not exactly," Clint said. "He said he knew who I was and had heard all about me from his wife. He emphasized those words. 'My . . . wife!' he said."

"Did he say anything else?"

"Yes, he told me that this was his time, and he was going to win the tournament."

"Why would he think you'd be interested in hearin' that?" Anne asked.

"I don't know," Clint said. "But he did."

She frowned.

"I don't like him warnin' you off," she said. "I mean, we're friends. If we see each other in town, we're going to talk."

"Right."

"Did you tell him we'd seen each other?"

"No."

"Still . . . I might be his wife, but that doesn't mean he owns me."

Her hair looked tousled, as if she had been lying down when he knocked. And her dress was slightly askew. She looked lovely as ever, but much sexier than when he had seen her that afternoon.

She saw the way he was looking at her.

"Do you . . . want to come in?" she asked.

Clint hesitated

"This is your room," he said after a beat.

"Yes."

"That you share with your husband."

"Yes."

"He could come back."

"Yes."

"Then no," he said, "I don't want to come in."

They stood there silently for a few moments, then she said. "The room across the hall is empty."

***

Clint would have forced the door of the empty room, but when she charged into his arms and they started kissing, she pushed him back against the door and it popped open.

After that they were on the bed.

Clint had kissed many women since he last kissed Anne Archer, but their lips fit together as if they had never stopped.

The smell and taste of her was so familiar, but the feel of her body was different. She was fuller, softer than she used to be, but maybe that was because she no longer spent so much time on a horse, hunting for outlaws.

After just lying on the bed together, kissing, for a few minutes, they started undoing each other's clothes, tossing items off in all directions until they were completely naked.

Now he was able to truly see how her body had matured during the years since he had last been with her. Her breasts and hips were fuller, delightfully so, her nipples even seemed to have gotten larger and darkened—unless he just didn't remember that fact very clearly.

"Oh, I'd forgotten," she said, taking his hard penis into her hands.

"What?" he asked, kissing her shoulders.

"How pretty you are."

She slithered down so she could rub the smooth column of flesh against her cheeks, then ran her lips and tongue over it. Finally, she rolled him onto his back and took him into her mouth.

He had forgotten how good she was at this. He looked down at her head bobbing up and down on him, wanted to settle back, relax and enjoy it, but then realized they didn't have that much time. So he reached down, slid his hands beneath her arms and pulled her up so that she was sitting on top of him.

"Impatient to be inside me?" she asked, with a beautiful smile.

"Exactly."

"Well," she said, "you won't have to wait any longer."

She raised her hips, reached between them to grasp him firmly and sat down on him again, letting him glide into her.

"Ohhhhhh," she groaned, closing her eyes, "somethin' else I forgot, how well you fit in me."

It was a perfect fit for him, too. He wondered suddenly what might have happened years ago if he had proposed to her. Would they have ridden around the country together, using their guns to support each other? Or could they have settled down somewhere and lived a normal life?

No, a normal life was something the Gunsmith had given up on, a long, long time ago.

"Hey." She slapped his chest. "Where'd you go?"

"Huh?"

"This is not very flatterin', you know?" she said. "I'm fuckin' you and you're fadin' away."

"Actually," he said, placing his hands on her hips as she rode him up and down, "I was thinking about you. About us."

She pressed both hands down onto his abdomen and asked, "Do you do that a lot? Think about me? Us?"

"Almost never."

She slapped his chest again, harder this time.

"Liar!"

"Ouch, you're right. I'm lying."

"Oh, just shut up and let me enjoy this," she said.

She closed her eyes, let her head fall back, and began to hop up and down on him faster and faster . . .

***

Later, Clint decided to make it up to her. He got her onto her back and gave her his complete attention.

"Now, that's more like it," she said, as he pressed his face between her legs.

"Quiet, woman," he said. "Pay attention."

As his tongue touched her she said, "Oh, don't worry, I will."

Chapter Fourteen

They would have liked to lay there together for a while, and then go again, but they both knew they couldn't do that.

"Don't feel bad about this," she said, as they got dressed.

"Why would I?"

"The man I used to know didn't like to sleep with married women," she pointed out.

"That man's long gone," he said. "Are you still the woman I knew?"

"Not at all," she said, smoothing down the front of her dress.

He strapped on his gun and faced her.

"Obviously, you're not happy in your marriage," he commented.

"I thought I was," she said. "I'd like to find out why I'm not, anymore."

"Why don't you ask him?"

"I did, several times," she said. "He always tells me I'm bein' silly."

"Okay," Clint said, "so I'll ask him."

"Just find out who he is, Clint," Anne said. "Find out who I actually married."

"And who you're going to divorce?"

"Probably."

***

Anne went back to her room, and Clint went to his hotel and turned in for the night.

In the morning he had a long breakfast, waiting for the games to start at the Buffalo, but he went to the Gold Rush, first.

"Wondered when you'd be back," Taft said.

"Been busy."

"Found your man?"

"Not yet."

"Still think he's in town?"

"I'm hoping."

"How about a beer? Or is it too early?"

"I thought you'd never ask and no, it's not."

Taft set a cold brew in front of him. Clint picked it up and looked around.

"No poker games?"

"No more qualifying games," Taft said. "Everybody's across the street. Now they're whittling the field down."

Clint nodded, drank some beer.

"I figured you'd be over there watchin' the games," Taft said.

"I will be," Clint said, "but I wanted one of your cold beers."

"Better than theirs, right?"

"Much," Clint drank some more. "So, I guess you haven't heard anything about my man?"

"Resnick, right?" Taft asked. "Big nose."

"That's him."

"Naw, nothin'. How much longer are you gonna look for him in town?"

"I should've left already," Clint said. "Tried to pick up his trail outside of town."

"So what's keepin' you here?"

"I ran into an old friend I wasn't expecting to see," Clint explained.

"A woman?"

"Oh, yeah."

"They usually make a man change his plans."

"I just agreed to do her a favor," Clint said. "Hopefully, it won't take me too long."

"And then you can go back to the other favor."

"Right."

"Another beer before you go?"

"Definitely!"

Chapter Fifteen

After two beers at the Gold Rush, Clint decided he needed to approach Abel Terrell head on. It was the only way he was going to get back to tracking Harry Resnick. He didn't want to have to tell Talbot Roper that he lost the man because of a woman—although Roper knew Clint's history with Anne Archer.

He crossed the street, walked between the two burly guards, and entered the Buffalo. There were less tables than last time, so things were progressing.

The bartender, Eddie, was leaning on his elbows on the bar, his chin in his hands, watching the action at the tables. When he saw Clint approaching he straightened up.

"How about a beer?" Clint said.

"Anythin' you want, Mr. Adams."

He brought it over, set it down, and stayed.

"Still in town, I see."

"Yep."

"And still no interest in playin' poker?"

"No."

"Just in the players, huh?"

"One player in particular."

"Oh," Eddie said. "That guy. The one who warned you away from his wife."

"You got that, too, huh?"

"I heard 'im."

It almost seemed to Clint all he had been doing since arriving in Kingman was drinking beer. He was going to have to take some action just to continue to move forward.

That meant finding out who and what this fellow Abel Terrell really was, so Anne Archer could get on with her life. He wondered, if she did, indeed, end up divorcing Terrell, if she would go back to bounty hunting.

That thought also gave Clint an idea, which he would pursue later at the telegraph office.

"Eddie, can you call Joi over?"

"Sure thing."

Eddie looked around, waved and Joi came walking over.

"Ah, Mr. Adams," she said, hands on her hips.

"Clint," he said.

"What can I do for you, Clint?" she asked.

"You've heard some of the conversations at the tables, haven't you?"

"Oh, yeah," she said. "The players talk among themselves, not even aware that we're here."

"And what about that table? Next to Bat Masterson's?" Clint asked.

"Sure, they talk."

"About what?"

"What they'll do after they win," she said. "That tall one . . ."

"Abel Terrell?"

"That's his name," she said. "He's desperate to win. And while he's been winnin', he's been braggin'."

"And who's at his table?" Clint asked.

"Nobody," she said. "That's what's funny. Wait until he has to sit at a table with some real poker players, like your friend Bat."

"And he doesn't pay any attention to you or the other girls?" Clint asked. There were two others, a black-haired, slender girl and a fairly large girl with red hair and breasts that looked as if they would spill from her bodice.

"Not to me," she said. "Leanne and Virginia are of the opinion that he doesn't like girls, 'cause he hasn't laid a hand on either of them. The other men, at least, reach out and stroke an arm or a thigh in appreciation as we go by."

"Maybe he just wants to pay strict attention to his cards," Clint said.

"I've watched lots of poker games in my time, Clint," Joi said, "and for him it won't matter. As soon as he's sittin' across from some real players, payin' attention to his cards won't help him."

"And how will he react to losing?" Clint asked.

She laughed.

"Badly," she said. "Very badly."

There were officials strolling the floor, watching the games, and now one shouted, "Two more players out. Combining tables!"

"It's gonna happen soon," she said. "The tables are less and less."

"Thanks, Joi."

"Anytime, Clint," she said. "Come and see me when you want to talk about somethin' else . . . like me."

"That's a promise," Clint said.

As Joi walked away Eddie leaned on the bar.

"So you know his wife?"

"I do," Clint said, "she's an old friend."

"And she didn't know about his . . . habit?"

"Apparently, not."

"Why is it always the bad players who get hooked on it?" Eddie asked.

"They're always chasing the dragon," Clint said. "He's been able to hide it from her this long, but no longer, I think."

"Then maybe," Eddie said, "she should see it, when it happens."

"No observers allowed," Clint pointed out. "No one but players."

Eddie shrugged.

"You're here," he reminded Clint. "And the boss said you get whatever you want."

"That's right," Clint said, "He did." He put his glass down and looked at Eddie. "You're a very smart man, Eddie."

Eddie straightened and said, "I'm just a bartender."

Chapter Sixteen

Clint was initially going to have Joi call Terrell over to the bar for him to confront, but now Eddie had given him a totally different idea. When the time came, when Terrell was placed at a table with Bat Masterson or Luke Short, he could just bring Anne in and let her watch her husband in action. There was no way he was going to beat either of those men, but he was going to try, and when he failed—according to Joi—he wouldn't react very well. And then she would see him for what he really was. It would help her make up her mind about her marriage.

Unless he had already helped her with that.

***

Harry Resnick looked up as the door opened and light came into the dingy interior of the shed he had been calling home for a couple of days.

"Is it time?" he asked, standing.

"No," his visitor said, "I brought you some more food and whiskey."

Resnick sat back down on the hard-wooden chair, his shoulders slumped. The visitor put the food and drink on the table in front of him.

"Got enough matches for the lamp?" he asked.

"Yeah, I got 'em," Resnick said. "Look, why can't I stay in a room in somebody's house? Maybe even a whorehouse—"

"The Gunsmith has been searching rooming houses and whorehouses," the visitor said. "You're better off here, believe me."

"What the hell is a man like the Gunsmith doin' trailin' me?" Resnick complained. "I knew somebody was on my back but I thought a lawman, or some kinda detective. Not the goddamned Gunsmith!"

"I told you," the visitor said, "he's just doin' a favor for a friend, some detective in Denver."

"Roper!" Resnick spat. "That bastard. Why don't he come for me himself?"

"Look," the visitor said, "it should only be a day or two before he gets bored and moves on. He's gonna be convinced you're not here, and that he'll have to pick up your trail again. Then you can relax."

"I need a change of clothes," Resnick complained. "These stink."

"And you need a bath," the visitor said. "But that'll all come later, I assure you. Just be patient."

"Yeah, patient."

The visitor turned to leave.

"You know," Resnick said, "there is somethin' that would help me to be more patient."

The visitor turned and looked at him.

"What is it? What do you want?"

"Well . . . a woman would be nice," Resnick said. "A saloon girl, even a whore. I don't care."

"The way you smell, in this shed?" the visitor asked. "With no bed? You really think a woman would come here?"

"Well, definitely make it a whore, then," Resnick said. "I mean, if you pay her—"

"If I pay her?"

"Okay," Resnick said, "I'll pay her."

"Look," the visitor said, "I'm not bringing a girl to this squalor. So just eat the food, drink the whiskey, and stay alive. Because if the Gunsmith finds you—"

"I know, I know," Resnick said, "he'll kill me. But why? I haven't done anythin' that's worth killin' for."

"Well," the visitor said, "that's going to be someone else's decision, isn't it?"

He turned, went out the door and left Resnick in the glow of the single lamp.

***

Anne Archer stood at the window of her room and looked down at the street. When she had arrived in Kingman with her husband, she hadn't been sure she was going to leave with him. Their brief marriage had, so far, not been what she had thought it would be.

Seeing Clint Adams, and being with him again, had confirmed her feeling that her marriage was over. But she still needed a legitimate reason, and she thought perhaps the gambling might be it.

Maybe Clint would succeed in helping her find what she needed to make the move and end the marriage, but she didn't know where she would go from there. She didn't necessarily think that Clint Adams was her answer. Perhaps going back to bounty hunting, but that would be going back, wouldn't it? Not moving on.

And wasn't that what life was about, moving on?

She moved away from the window and sat on the bed, thinking about her old partners, Sandy Spillane and Katy Littlefeather, and wondering what they were doing at that very moment?

Chapter Seventeen

Clint decided to leave the Buffalo, let the games continue until the tables were down to a precious few. Meanwhile, he would go and send the telegrams he had been thinking about.

It didn't take long to write them out and get them sent. Hopefully, Rick Hartman from Labyrinth, Texas would find him what he wanted, or one of the other telegrams would come through for him.

As he left the telegraph office thinking about his next move, a man came walking up to him.

"Are you Mister Adams?" he asked.

"I am."

He was in his 30s, wearing a gun on his hip and a deputy's badge on his clean shirt.

"Sheriff Hoskins sent me to tell you, sir, that he thinks he's found your man. Resnick, is it?"

"That's right. Where is he?"

"I'm to give you directions."

"Why not just take me there?" Clint asked.

"That's what I said," the deputy answered. "But the sheriff wants me to make my regular rounds first."

"Okay," Clint said, "then direct me."

***

The directions were pretty simple to follow. They took him to an empty lot a couple blocks off the main street, where the deputy told him the sheriff would be waiting. But when he arrived no one was there. He looked around, saw dilapidated houses that appeared abandoned, and some sheds. Maybe Resnick was hiding in one of them. While he was waiting for the sheriff to arrive, he figured he would have a look. In fact, maybe the lawman wasn't even coming. Maybe this was just his way of showing Clint where Resnick was.

He walked over to a row of four houses, all apparently empty, with broken fences and gates, shutters hanging from windows like broken wings.

He went up onto the battered porch of the first house, entered through the open front door. It was small, so it didn't take long to look around and see it was empty. In fact, he could see that no one had been there for a long time.

He left that house and started over to the second. It was much the same, broken down and empty. But as he came out the door, there was a shot and a chunk of lead imbedded itself in the wall right next to his head.

Clint ducked back through the front door of the house, went to one of the broken windows to try and spot the shooter. Whoever it was had rushed his shot, instead of waiting until Clint was out in the open. And even so, the bullet had come very close to his head.

He kept his own gun holstered, as there was nothing yet to shoot at. Peering out the broken window he saw some outbuildings across the way, leantos and sheds, one of which had to be hiding a shooter. So he watched, and waited.

In the meantime, he had to decide if the sheriff had been involved in setting him up for an ambush, or if his name had simply been used to get Clint there. He didn't know if the man who had given him the message actually was a deputy, but he certainly had been wearing a badge.

Clint started to wonder if the shooter had shot and ran. One shot, which missed, and then he lit out? That wasn't much of an ambush.

He left the window and went to the door. The only way to find out was to go and see if the shooter tried again.

Slowly, he moved out the door, watching intently for any movement across the street. He'd been wrong. The shooter hadn't run, he had been incredibly patient. Now that Clint was outside, the man stepped from behind an old outhouse and began firing—multiple shots, this time, not one.

Clint dove off the porch rather than duck into the house. There was nothing to be accomplished in there. The action was outside.

When Clint hit the ground, he rolled and came up with his gun in hand. There was no cover in front of the house, but the shots stopped as the assailant had to reload. That gave Clint a chance to scramble from the house's front yard to a horse trough located just outside the fence.

A couple of shots slammed into the trough, punching holes in it so that water started running out the other side. Clint peered over the top to see where the shooter was. At that point the man stepped out with his rifle and fired another shot. Clint fired once, catching the shooter in the shoulder. He dropped his rifle, grabbed his shoulder, and this time he did turn and run.

Clint moved out from behind the horse trough and started after him. But the shooter was a fast runner, and he knew the streets and alleys of the town better than Clint. After only a few blocks, he lost him.

Clint returned to the scene of the shooting and picked up the fallen rifle. It was a Winchester, several years old, in good working condition. It made him think of the gun rack in Sheriff Hoskins' office.

Carrying the gun, he headed for the sheriff's office to find out just how involved Hoskins was.

Chapter Eighteen

Clint entered the sheriff's office, slammed the rifle down on his desk and asked, "Is this yours?"

Hoskins looked up at him in surprise, then over at the gun rack on the wall.

"See for yourself."

Clint looked at the rack. Shotguns and rifles, none of which were missing.

"What's this about?"

"You got a young, clean-shaven deputy who looks like he doesn't drink yet?" Clint asked.

"No," Hoskins said, "I have two experienced men in their thirties, and they drink plenty."

"Are you missing any deputy badges?"

"Only got two, and they're both bein' worn."

Clint stared at him.

"Coffee? Or whiskey?"

"Whiskey," Clint said. "Somebody just tried to kill me."

Hoskins took a bottle and two glasses out of his desk drawer.

"Have a seat and tell me about it."

Clint did.

***

When he was done Hoskins picked up the rifle.

"It looks like it could've come from my rack," But it didn't," he said.

"And the guy I shot?"

"The description could fit anybody," the lawman said, "but I'll check with the doctor."

"Is there anybody else in town who could treat a gun-shot wound?" Clint asked.

"A couple," the sheriff said. "I'll check with them, too."

"It probably doesn't matter," Clint said. "I'll bet he has a friend who can remove a bullet—if it even stayed in. It might have gone right through. Then they just have to stop the bleeding."

"So you don't want me to look?"

"I'd rather you look for the phony deputy," Clint said.

"And he was wearin' a badge, you say?"

Clint nodded.

"And it looked real."

"Did it look . . . old?"

"Now that you mention it," Clint said. "He was shiny and new, but the badge wasn't."

Hoskins opened another drawer and looked inside.

"What?"

"There was an old badge in here that I don't use anymore," he said, closing the drawer. "It's missing." He looked at the gun rack. "They probably would've taken a gun if they could've got the lock open."

"Great. This has got to be about Resnick."

"Why?" Hoskins asked. "Why not just somebody who recognized you and decided to ambush you?"

"This was planned," Clint said. "The badge, the phone, deputy, the location. If somebody wanted to get credit for killing the Gunsmith, they'd do it in front of people."

"So Resnick knows somebody in town," Hoskins said. "This was his destination."

"He's still here," Clint said, staring at the whiskey glass he was holding but had not yet sipped from.

"I was hopin' you'd decide he wasn't and leave town before somethin' like this happened."

"Well," Clint said, "that's not going to happen now." He drank the whiskey, set the glass down on Hoskins' desk, and stood up.

"You find the phony deputy and your stolen badge," he said, "and I'll find Resnick."

"Adams—"

"It'll be easier if we split the tasks," Clint said. "I can talk to the town doc."

"Doc Grady, down the street."

Clint nodded, turned and went out.

***

"Shoulder wound," Doc Grady said.

It sounded like an older man's name, so Clint had expected a grizzled old sawbones. Instead, he found a handsome woman in her 40s, wearing a white coat and looking very fetching in it. She had dark hair tied up in a bun behind her head.

When he knocked she had let him in, asked if she could help. She didn't have a patient at the moment, so he told her about the man he had shot.

"Right shoulder," he said.

"I haven't treated anyone like that today," she told him. "Have you told the sheriff?"

"I have," Clint said. "He suggested I check with you."

"That's our sheriff," she said. "Never do for himself what he can get someone else to do."

They were in a small sitting room with a desk and several chairs.

"Anything else?" she asked, "I am expecting some patients."

"If you do have a patient like that, would you let me know?"

"What hotel are you staying at?" she asked.

"I couldn't get into a hotel," he said. "I've got a room upstairs from the Gold Rush Saloon."

"You're staying with a—"

"No," he said, "Taft, the owner, is letting me use a room."

"I see," she said. "Well, all right. If I have a patient with a shoulder wound, I'll let you know."

"One more thing," Clint said. "Who else in town can sew up bullet wounds?"

"You want me to tell you who my competition is?"

"No," Clint said, "I'd like you to tell me who a wounded man would go to if he didn't want to be seen coming here."

"I'll give you three names," she said, "and then you have to leave. Deal?"

"Deal."

She gave him the names.

"Thank you, Doc."

"Doctor," she said. "I'm trying to get the people in this town to call me Doctor."

"Thank you, Doctor. I look forward to hearing from you."

He turned and left, passing a patient who was limping in. He had two good shoulders.

Chapter Nineteen

The first name was Douglas Weems.

Weems had a shop on Drinkwater Street, where he sold tarpaulins and lumber and other building equipment. Doc Grady also said that he had experience during the war removing bullets and sewing up wounded soldiers when there was no doctor.

Clint entered the shop and looked around. It was empty.

"Weems!" Clint yelled. "Douglas Weems!"

He waited, was about to call out again when a man came from a back room. He was stocky, medium height, and in his 60s. He was wiping his hands on a grimy cloth.

"You need somethin'?" the man asked.

"The sheriff sent me over to ask you if you've patched up any bullet wounds lately," Clint said.

He stopped wiping his hands.

"I ain't a doctor."

"Yeah, but you know how to remove a bullet and sew a wound," Clint said.

"Who told you that?"

"The sheriff."

"Well," Weems said, "I done it once or twice."

"Lately?"

"No."

"If someone comes in with a bullet hole in his shoulder, the sheriff would like to know."

"I'll tell 'im."

"You do that."

Clint turned to leave.

"Hey!"

He turned.

"Who are you?"

"The name's Clint Adams."

Weems raised his eyebrows.

"I heard you was in town."

"And I plan to be for some time," Clint said, and left.

***

The second name was Mary Cassidy. She had a dress shop on Main Street. When he walked in an older woman in her 60s was sitting on a chair, sewing a dress.

"Can I help you, sir?" she asked. "Do you need a dress for your wife?"

"You're pretty good with that needle and thread," Clint said.

"It's my business."

"Have you used it to sew up any bullet wounds?" Clint asked.

She stopped sewing and looked up at him.

"I have, on occasion," she said.

"Anyone lately?"

"Lately?" she asked. "Who wants to know?"

"The sheriff."

"Why didn't you say so? I've sewed up a bullet hole or two, but nothin' lately. Why would they come to me when they got Doc Grady?"

"Maybe they don't like Doctor Grady."

"She's had trouble gettin' accepted here because she's a woman," Mary Cassidy said. "Why would one of those people come to me?"

"Is she from here?" Clint asked.

"No," Mary said, "she came here a few months ago, after old Doc Milburn died."

"But you're from here?"

"I am."

"Then maybe that'd be the difference," Clint suggested.

"Maybe. You try Doug Weems?"

"I did," Clint said.

"Well," she said, "if I see anybody like that, I'll let the sheriff know."

"That's all we want," Clint said. "Thank you."

"Don't mention it."

She went back to her sewing, never asked Clint if he was a deputy, or even who he was.

Chapter Twenty

The third name was Coley Burns.

Coley was a bartender in a small saloon called The Spur. Doc Grady told Clint that he had been known to serve a beer and sew up a wound at the same time.

"Of course," she added, "this could just be talk."

Clint decided to find out.

He entered The Spur Saloon, was not surprised to find it very cramped inside, with a bar, and about three tables which, at the moment, were not in use. The two men standing at the bar eyed him suspiciously, and as he approached they both put their beers down and left.

"Sorry if that was my fault," he told the bartender.

"Forget it," the bartender said. "They're the nervous types. What'll ya have?"

"A beer and some information, if you're Coley Burns."

The tall, gangly man in his 40s studied Clint for a few moments, then said, "I am."

"Let's start with the beer, then."

Coley nodded, drew the beer and set it on the bar in front of Clint.

"What kind of questions?" he asked.

"Actually, just one or two. I've heard stories about you sewing men up. Their wounds, I mean."

"Oh, that," Coley said. "That story about me sewing a guy up and servin' him a beer at the same time?"

"That's the one."

"Why's that interest you?"

"Because," Clint said, truthfully, "I shot a man and I'm trying to find out if he was treated by somebody other than the doctor."

"Well," Coley said, "the story's true. I did do that. It was either that or have the guy bleed all over my bar."

"Ah," Clint said, "that makes sense."

"But I ain't done nothin' like that in a long while," Coley added. "Sorry, I ain't your guy."

Clint took a few swallows of beer. It was lukewarm.

"Okay, then, thanks," he said, putting it down.

"Don't want the rest of it?"

"No thanks."

"Still gotta charge ya full price."

"No problem."

"Four bits."

"For lukewarm beer?"

"Two bits for the beer, two bits for the question."

Clint stared at Burns for a few moments, then decided, "that's fair," and paid.

***

Clint left The Spur and went back to the Buffalo. He walked to the bar, looking over at the tables. There were less, but Bat, Luke and Terrell were still sitting at separate ones.

"How's it goin'?" Eddie asked.

"Somebody tried to kill me," Clint said. "I guess that means I'm getting somewhere."

"Beer? Or do you need a whiskey?"

"Just beer. A cold one."

"Have you had any other kind here?" Eddie asked.

"No, but I just had a lukewarm one at The Spur."

Eddie made a face as he set the beer down.

"What were you doin' there?"

"Looking for somebody who could sew up a bullet wound."

"That story about Coley Burns? That can't be true."

"He claims it is."

"Hogwash."

At that moment Big Bill Bartlett came walking over.

"Hey, boss," Eddie said. "Beer?"

"Thanks, Eddie." He looked at Clint. "Find your man?"

"Not yet," Clint said, "but I must be getting close without knowing it."

"How's that?"

"Somebody took a few shots at me today," Clint said.

"An ambush?"

"More than that," Clint said. "It was a set-up."

"Who set you up?"

"A young man who claimed to be a deputy," Clint said. "Real fresh-faced type."

"He had a badge?"

Clint nodded.

"An old one the sheriff used to have in his desk."

"That Hoskins," Big Bill said. "He should've been replaced a long time ago."

"That's the town's problem, not mine," Clint said. "He's going to try and find the phony deputy."

"So he says."

"Well, I put a bullet in the shooter's shoulder," Clint said. "He didn't see Doc Grady."

"There's other folks in town can remove a bullet."

"So I've been told," Clint said. "I've talked to three, but they claim nobody's come to them."

"One of them could be lying."

"That's what I've been thinking."

"Any ides which one?"

"I have a hunch I'm going to follow up on."

Chapter Twenty-One

Clint remained in the Buffalo for a good portion of the evening, preferring to pursue his hunch in the light the next day. The darkness would make it too easy to ambush him, now that the setup had not worked.

With the tables remaining the same for the last two hours he was there, he decided to go across to the Gold Rush and turn in.

He stopped to exchange a few words with Taft at the bar, but declined another beer.

"I got three girls workin' here," Taft said, "either one of them would like to come up and make you more comfortable."

"I appreciate the offer, Taft," Clint said, "but I think I'm just going to get some sleep."

"Suit yerself," Taft said. "They're good girls."

"I'm sure they are."

He bade goodnight to Taft and went upstairs.

***

He was in the room for an hour when there was a knock on the door. He had decided to do a little reading before turning in, but found that he had been drifting off with the book on his chest when the knock woke him.

Sure that it was one of Taft's girls he, nevertheless, took his gun to the door with him.

"Who is it?"

He was surprised when a woman's voice said, "Doctor Grady."

He opened the door. That afternoon he had seen her in a white coat. Now he saw that she probably had this same black suit on underneath it.

"Doctor," Clint said, "did you think of something to tell me?"

"I did," she said, "if I can come in?"

Clint looked down at her black medicine bag dangling from her left hand.

"Oh, this," she said, lifting it. "I told the bartender I was visiting you in a professional capacity. Having this with me supported that."

"I see," Clint said. "Well, come in, then. You seem to have your reputation covered,"

She walked past him into the room. He closed the door, then walked to the bedpost and put his gun back in his holster.

"What's on your mind, Doctor?" he asked, turning to face her.

They could hear music coming from downstairs, and the sound of voices. That had been another reason Clint had not gone right to sleep.

"On second thought," she said, "I think you should come with me."

"Where are we going?" he asked.

"Someplace we can talk where there's not so much noise."

"And where's that?"

"My office."

"Is this important, Doctor?"

"Hey," she said, "you came to me, remember? Asking for my help? Well, now I think I can give it to you."

Clint sighed, sat down on the bed.

"All right, just let me get my boots back on."

***

As Clint and Doctor Grady walked past the bar Taft gave him a little salute.

It was dark out, with the street lamps throwing shadows that a man with a rifle could easily hide in. But Clint didn't think Doctor Grady was trying to set him up.

"I guess you don't mind walking around town at night," Clint said.

"I'm the only doctor in town," she said. "Maybe there's a few others, like I told you, who can remove a bullet, but they need me for every other ailment. I don't think anybody's going to try to hurt me." She looked over her shoulder at him. "Besides, I've got the Gunsmith with me. How much safer can I be?"

They reached her office and he waited while she unlocked the door.

"I'll go first, to light a lamp," she said.

"Be my guest," he said. "Ladies first, anyway."

"Right," she said.

She went into the dark confines of the office, and moments later Clint saw the light and entered, closing the door behind him.

"Make sure you lock that, please," she said.

"Got it."

He locked it.

"Come in," she said, and went through another door.

He followed her, found that they were in the room she used to treat her patients. There was counter space for her instruments, reflectors to increase the intensity of the light coming from the lamps, an examining table and, in the corner, a bed.

"In case I need to keep a patient here overnight," she told him, seeing what he was looking at.

"I get it."

"Just wait here a minute," she said. "I have to go into this other room."

"Okay."

She went through a door and he stood there, wondering if he should stand or sit. He went over to the counter to look at her medical instruments. He didn't know what anything was called, but he could figure out that one was to take a bullet out, and another was to cauterize a wound.

He heard the door open behind him, turned and froze.

"What's wrong?" she asked.

She was wearing the white coat he had seen her in that morning, but . . . nothing else. Her long, bare legs were pale and shapely.

"Well . . ." he said.

"Why did you think I asked you back here?"

"I thought you had something to tell me about the man who was shot."

"Sorry," she said, "I just have something to show you."

With that she opened her coat.

Chapter Twenty-Two

Her breasts were large, firm, with full undersides and large, brown nipples.

"Any objection to me taking this off?" she asked, holding the coat open with both hands.

"No," he said, after licking his lips, "no objections."

"I didn't think so."

She removed the coat completely and tossed it aside.

"That bed is going to be used for something other than a patient tonight," she told him, walking to it.

"Doctor Grady—"

"I appreciate you calling me Doctor, Mr. Adams, but for tonight I think you should call me Louise. Or Lou."

"All right . . . Lou."

"And may I call you Clint?"

"I think you better."

"Get your clothes off, Clint," she said. "And get rid of that gun."

"I'll have to keep it close by."

"You think I'm going to try to hurt you?" she asked, with a smile.

"Not you," he said. "Somebody's already taken a shot at me."

There were two chairs in the room. She took one and placed it near the bed.

"Hang it there," she suggested.

He undid his gunbelt and hung it over the back of the chair. She took the opportunity to press up against him and kiss him. He slid his hands down her smooth back until he could cup the cheeks of her backside.

She broke the kiss long enough to say, "Mmmm, now you're getting interested."

"Can't help it," he said, as the heat of her body went right through his clothing.

"Mmm," she said, kissing him again. "I think we need to get rid of some of these clothes."

She unbuttoned his shirt, slid her hands inside and rubbed his chest before sliding it off of him. After that she unbuckled his belt and unbuttoned his trousers, all the while still kissing him. She tugged the pants down over his hips, and they stuck there as she reached inside his underwear and grabbed his hardening penis.

"Yes," she said, stroking him, "*very* interested."

He grabbed her then, held her tightly and kissed her, with *great* interest.

"Okay," she said, putting her hands on his chest and pushing, "let's get these off."

She turned him, pushed him into a seated position on the edge of the bed, and then removed his boots, socks and trousers. He lifted his hips to allow her to remove his underwear, and then she got on her knees in front of him and began to kiss his cock.

She cradled him in both hands and ran her lips and tongue over him, then abruptly took the entire length of him into her mouth. She seemed to be touching spots with the tip of her tongue that he had never had touched before, and he wondered if it was her knowledge as a doctor at work?

He was almost at the point of exploding into her mouth when she gripped him tightly with one hand and allowed him to pop free. His urge to ejaculate died down, and she stood and slid into his lap, pinning his hard cock between them. She then used her weight to bear him down onto his back. Clint wondered if this desire for sex had been with her that morning when they met, or if it had just come over her this evening?

Once she was on his lap she moved her hips and took him into the steaming, wet depth of her pussy. She started to ride him, slowly at first, and then faster and faster. All the while she was doing something with her muscles that made him feel as if he was being gripped by a fist.

He decided to take his time and enjoy this. There didn't seem to be any chance that someone would walk in on them. Of course, since she was the town sawbones, somebody could always come to the door with an emergency, but for the time being it was just the two of them.

Placing his hands on her hips, he matched her tempo, bringing his butt up off the bed every time she came down on him. Soon they were both grunting from the effort, comingling with the sound of their flesh slapping together.

He didn't get tired of her riding him, not when her breasts were bouncing around in front of his face, but finally decided to take action and change their positions. She was not a small woman, but he managed to lift her off of him so that his penis came out, then slipped her onto her back, so they could change places. Now he was on top, and slid his hard cock right back into her wet pussy with ease.

"Oh God," she said, wrapping her legs around his waist, "I really need this. Come on, do it to me hard."

"I'll give you what you want," he promised.

He unwrapped her legs from around him, took an ankle in each hand, spread her wide and then started fucking her as hard as he could. He grunted out loud every time he drove into her, and her eyes widened with each stroke. He knew he was giving her what she wanted because she was not only taking it, but asking for more.

"Come on," she gasped, "come on, come on . . ."

He kept coming on!

Chapter Twenty-Three

Propped up on his elbow, Clint circled her nipples with his forefinger while she laid on her back. Her breasts, while large, were remarkably firm and didn't sag to the sides like some women's did when lying on their back.

"You're quite a woman, Lou," he said. "That didn't sound right. I think I'll call you Louise, instead."

"Unless we're around other people," she said, "then I'd still like you to call me Doctor Grady."

"You have a deal, Louise," Clint said.

He leaned over, kissed one nipple, then the other. Louise sighed and cradled his head with one arm. He kissed her smooth skin, working his way down her body until he was finally down between her legs.

"Whoa, wait," she said, pushing his head away and drawing her knees up. "What are you doing?"

"I was just kissing . . . I was going to kiss you—"

"Not there!" she said. "That French stuff is dirty."

"But, since you took me in your mouth, I thought—"

"Nobody's ever done that to me," she said. "I . . . I don't know . . ."

"Louise, I'm—"

"I think you better go." She grabbed the bedsheet and pulled it up to cover herself. Suddenly, she was a totally different woman.

He got out of bed and started to get dressed. Dr. Grady obviously had some . . . problems he didn't know about.

"All right," he said, strapping on his gun. "Louise, I'm sorry."

"It's Doctor Grady, Mr. Adams," she said. "Please remember that."

He started for the door, then stopped and turned.

"Doctor Grady, did you, uh, have anything to tell me?" Clint asked. "Is that why you came to me?"

"No," she said, curled up on the bed and not looking at him, "nothing. I just . . . needed some sex."

"I see."

She turned her head to look at him.

"It's not going to happen again."

"No," he said, "it's not," and left.

***

As he walked back to his hotel he felt that he really couldn't be angry with her. Not all women liked what he had been about to do to her. It was just odd that she would balk at that, yet do what she did to him. She was a mature, professional woman, but apparently she still had some things she wouldn't do.

But most people did.

This had just been a mistake.

Chapter Twenty-Four

He came down the next morning and accepted a cup of coffee from Taft. The three girls—Darla, Bonnie and Lily—were at their table, called out "Good morning," cheerily.

"I appreciate the room, Taft, but I'd also appreciate it if you didn't let anyone go up there."

"You talkin' about Doc Grady?" Taft asked. "She had her bag with her. I figured it was, you know, professional."

"Well," Clint said, "I'm not expecting anyone, professional or otherwise."

"Then what was it about?"

Clint sipped his coffee.

"I'm still trying to figure that out," he admitted.

"We got eggs comin' out," Taft said. "You interested?"

"Thanks, but no," Clint said. "I'll get something down the street. I want to check in with the sheriff, first."

"Suit yourself," Taft said. "I don't have much faith in the local law."

"I've heard that from others, as well," Clint said, "but he's the only law I've got to work with."

"I dunno how much help you're gonna get from him," Taft said. "If I was you, I'd watch myself."

"Thanks for the advice," Clint said, setting the empty cup down, "and the coffee."

Clint left the saloon.

***

Instead of heading for the sheriff's office, though, Clint went to Anne Archer's hotel and knocked on the door of her room.

"Breakfast?" he asked when she opened the door.

"I was just on my way out." The way she was dressed made that obvious, but it was still in a dress, something he wasn't used to seeing her in. She looked pretty in it, but she belonged in trail clothes, with a gun on her hip.

"Let's go, then," he said.

She stepped out into the hall, pulled the door shut, made sure it was locked, then followed him down to the lobby.

"Your husband?" he asked, as they got outside.

"Already gone to his game," she said. "Have you been over there?"

"I have."

"How's he doing?" she asked.

"Won't he tell you?"

"No."

"He's doing well."

"Can he win?"

"Sure, he *can*," Clint said.

"Is he going to?"

"No."

"How do you know that?"

"Because Bat Masterson and Luke Short are involved," Clint said.

"So one of them is gonna win?"

"Yes."

"How can you be so sure?"

"History."

"Which tells you what?"

"That when Bat doesn't win, Luke does," Clint said, "and when Luke doesn't win, Bat does."

"So you've never beat one of them?"

"No."

They reached the small café where he had previously eaten a steak and went inside. It wasn't busy, so he got the table he wanted.

"I don't do this anymore," she said.

"What?"

"Sit with my back to the wall."

"You're not hunting bounty anymore, so you think you're safe from backshooters?"

"Nobody is safe from backshooters," she said, "it's just that nobody has a reason to, anymore."

"Old enemies," he commented.

"I think I've been out of the business long enough," Anne said.

"I hope so."

They ordered breakfast and Anne asked, "What about the reason you came to town? Did you find your man, yet?"

"No," he said, "but he's here. I'll find him."

"Do you want some help?" she asked. "I still have some of my old skills."

"That's okay," Clint said. "I've got it covered. I have an idea."

She shrugged.

"It's just this sittin' around, doesn't feel right to me," she complained.

"Shouldn't be too much longer," Clint said. "This tournament should be down to two or three tables pretty soon. Your man's going to find the competition a lot stiffer."

"Is he one of those gamblers who thinks he's better than he is?" she asked.

"Looks like it."

"Is there any chance I'd be able to come in and watch?"

"As it happens," Clint said, "I'm working on that very idea."

Chapter Twenty-Five

After breakfast Clint told Anne Archer he had to see the sheriff.

"I guess I'll go back to my hotel and sit in my room," she said. "There's not much else I can do."

"I'll let you know what's happening at the game," he promised.

"I appreciate it, Clint," she said. "And if you have time, maybe we can put that empty room to good use, again."

"Anne," he said, "you're a married woman."

"That didn't seem to bother you last time," she pointed out.

"Let's talk about it later," he offered.

"Sure," she said. "Thanks for breakfast."

She turned and walked off down the street toward her hotel. Clint watched, knowing that her being a married woman was not going to keep him from her if she offered again. After all, she was Anne Archer, the woman who occupied the back of his mind, constantly.

He turned, crossed the street and headed for the sheriff's office.

"Not a word," Hoskins said, when Clint entered. "Ain't seen or heard a thing."

"Tell me about Douglas Weems."

"Weems?" The sheriff frowned at the question. "Didn't you talk to him, yourself?"

"Yes," Clint said. "He seems the likely one to have treated my shooter."

"Yeah? Why?"

"Just the feeling I got after talking to all three of the people you gave me," Clint said. "That is, unless there's somebody else we don't know about."

"That ain't likely."

"What do you know about him, then?"

"Not much," Hoskins said. "He sells building equipment."

"Has he always done that?"

"He's tried lots of different things," Hoskins said. "Used to have a leather shop, then a hardware store. Can't seem to keep 'em goin'."

"Well, the store he has now doesn't look too prosperous, either," Clint said. "Maybe he's making his money in other ways."

"Like what?"

"Like patching up men who don't want to go to the doctor," Clint said.

"Look," Hoskins said, "all I told you is that he's got the know-how, learned it in the war. If he's doin' it—"

"I'll find out," Clint said. "He'd need a place to do it, and the back of his store would fit the bill."

"Why are you tellin' me?" Hoskins asked, fidgeting behind his desk.

"I've been hearing things about you, Sheriff Hoskins," Clint said.

"What kinda things?"

"Like you might not be real good at your job."

"I do the best I can."

"Have you found out yet who stole that badge you're missing?"

"No," Hoskins said, "but I will."

"Good," Clint said. "With you following that angle, we're bound to catch whoever it was took that shot at me. Or even who put him up to it."

"That's the plan," Hoskins said. "Maybe you shouldn't be listenin' to gossip around town about the local law."

"Maybe I shouldn't," Clint agreed. "See you later, Sheriff."

"Adams."

Clint left the man's office.

***

After Clint had sent his telegrams he asked the clerk to hold onto any replies.

As he walked in the telegraph clerk acknowledged him with a wave of his hand.

"Got them replies you was waitin' for," he said, handing them over.

"That's good. Thanks."

"Yessir."

"Do I owe you anything?"

"No sir, not a thing," the clerk said. He was nervous, so he obviously knew who Clint was.

"Well, here," Clint said, handing him a dollar. "Thanks, again."

"Yes, sir, thank *you*."

Clint stepped outside, where there was a wooden bench against the front of the office. He sat and went through the telegrams. Both were from Rick Hartman, each on a different subject. With the information they gave him, he went back inside and sent two more.

Chapter Twenty-Six

The telegrams were for Anne Archer's benefit, but he didn't want to tell her about them, yet. The results might not turn out to be what he was hoping for. So for now, he kept them to himself.

He walked to Douglas Weems' shop, peered in the front window. Weems was behind the counter, leaning with his chin in his hand, reading something.

Clint went around the building to the back, found that the door there was flimsy enough for him to force without much noise. He entered and found himself in a back room crowded with a large, wooden work table and plenty of building materials. He quickly searched, looking for anything that would indicate that someone who had been shot had been there, recently.

There was nothing.

Weems could have treated the shooter and then cleaned up, but from the looks of the place, cleaning up wasn't high on his list. If he had treated a wounded man, there would be some indication.

He went to the doorway that led to the main part of the shop. Weems was still in the same position. He decided he had time to search again, more thoroughly.

This time he moved some of the building equipment, doing it as silently as he could. He moved a barrel that felt empty, was about to look inside when he saw the stain on the floor. He set the barrel aside and knelt down. It was red—or had been when it first hit the floor. Now it was a darker color, having soaked in, but there was no doubt that it was blood.

He turned and walked into the shop. Weems straightened when he saw him, looking confused.

"What the hell—"

"I've got something to show you," Clint said.

"What are you—"

"Back here," Clint said. "Come on."

He turned and went back into the storeroom.

"Hey, you can't do that," Weems shouted, following him in. "You ain't allowed—"

"You really should clean up better back here, Douglas," Clint said.

"Yeah, well—whataya mean—"

"I mean this," Clint said, using the point of his boot to indicate the stain on the floor.

"Oh, that—that's just—"

"Blood."

"Yeah, well, I, uh, cut myself—"

"Must've been pretty bad," Clint said. "Let's see it."

"I, uh, can't it's, uh, bandaged—"

"You can't show it to me because you didn't cut your-self," Clint said. "This blood is from a man you treated for a gunshot wound."

Weems looked around nervously, then seemed to steel himself.

"Well, so what?" he asked. "A man's gotta right to make some money on the side, ain't he?"

"He does," Clint said. "Unless it's for bushwhacking somebody."

"I didn't bushwhack nobody!"

"No," Clint said, "you just treated a bushwhacker."

"How was I supposed to know—"

"Who was he?"

"I—I don't know," Weems said. "He came here, bleedin' from a bullet wound—"

"Where?"

"What?"

"Was he shot in the shoulder?"

"Well, yeah, but—how'd you know that?"

"Because I'm the one who shot him," Clint said, "when he tried to kill me."

"Oh."

"So I need to know everything you know, Weems," Clint said. "And I mean everything."

When Clint left Douglas Weems' shop he had a description, and that was all. No matter how he pressed Weems, the man said he didn't know the wounded man's name. And he didn't know who had sent him.

"He's tall," Clint said to Taft, "slender, in his thirties, with sandy hair."

"That could match a lot of guys," Taft said. "Why ain't you tellin' the sheriff?"

"I don't trust him," Clint said. "Didn't you tell me he wasn't good at his job?"

"Did I say that?"

"Well . . . is he?"

"Useless," Taft said.

Clint had considered going to the sheriff with the shooter's description, but at the last minute he had changed direction and gone to the Gold Rush to talk to Taft. If anyone had seen a man like that around town, it would be a bartender.

"That's why I came to you," Clint said.

"Let me think about it," Taft said. "Maybe I'll come up with . . . someone."

"Meanwhile," Clint said, "I'll have one more beer before I go upstairs."

Chapter Twenty-Seven

When the knock came at his door Clint was almost drifting off to sleep while reading. He grabbed his gun, since he had asked Taft not to let anyone come up to the room.

"Who is it?"

"It's Lily," a girl's voice said, "from downstairs."

Lily. He remembered the name, but not which girl she was. When he opened the door he saw a little blonde standing there, still wearing her dress from earlier in the evening.

"Lily," he said, recognizing her. "What can I do for you?"

"Taft has somethin' to show you, Mr. Adams," Lily said. "He asked me to bring you."

"Where?" Clint asked. "I was about to turn in."

"It's just down the hall," Lily said. "If you'll follow me? You won't even need your gun."

"Lily," he said, "I always need my gun." "Well, all right," she said. "I'm sorry. Of course, bring your gun. Like I said, it's just down the hall."

Clint didn't have his boots on, but since Lily was only taking him down the hall, he followed in his socks, with his gun tucked into his belt.

"It's just down here," Lily said, leading him to a closed door.

Since there had already been an attempt to bushwhack him, Clint wasn't about to just walk blindly into that room. He stopped.

"Is there a problem?" Lily asked.

"That depends on what's waiting for me on the other side of this door," Clint told her.

"It's nothin' bad," she said. "I swear."

She seemed very sincere, but still . . .

"Then you go in first," he said.

"No problem."

She opened the door and entered the room. He followed close behind, prepared for anything.

Anything but what he got.

Inside the room the other two girls, Darla and Bonnie, were sitting on the bed, still in their dresses. Taft, the bartender, was nowhere to be seen.

Lily closed the door behind them.

"What's this?" Clint asked.

"Taft said you need to relax," Lily said. "Bonnie, Darla and me, we're gonna help you do that."

"Now girls," Clint said, "if you're thinking of doing this because Taft told you to, it isn't necessary."

Bonnie stood up, slipped her dress off her shoulders and let it drop to the floor. She was naked, with full breasts and hips on glorious display, and the prerequisite number of freckles a redhead is supposed to have.

"Taft don't make us do anythin' we don't wanna," she assured him.

"That's true," the brunette, Darla, said.

She stood up and shrugged her dress off, revealing herself to be slender, pale and lovely, small breasts tipped by brown nipples.

He heard a familiar sound from behind him—the rustling of fabric on skin—turned and saw Lily's dress falling to the floor. She was smaller than the other two girls, very pale, the hair between her legs even blonder than the hair on her head. The nipples on the tips of her small, solid looking breasts were pink.

"The girls are right, Mr. Adams," she said. "We only do what we want to."

As they surrounded him, putting their hands on him, heat emanating from their naked bodies, he felt himself beginning to stir.

***

The 3 women undressed him.

He had been with 2 a time or two in the past, but not 3. He decided to just let them have their way, but still kept his gun close to the bed.

In fact, he jammed a chair under the doorknob before turning himself over to them.

"You don't trust us?" Lily asked, with a pretty pout.

"Just playing it safe," he assured her.

He kissed her first, just to keep her happy.

When the girls had Clint completely undressed and naked they drew him to the bed and laid him down on his back. They joined him on the bed, Bonnie pressing her full breasts to his face while Lily and Darla scooted down to pay attention to his hard, raging penis.

While he ran his tongue over Bonnie's breasts and nipples, the other girls ran their tongues up and down his hard cock, and then Lily took it into her mouth and began sucking. The other girl, Darla, started licking his testicles.

It went on like that for some time until Bonnie decided to make a change. She climbed atop Clint's chest, pressing her fragrant pussy to his face. At the same time Lily straddled him, held his hard cock so she could slide down on it, taking it inside.

Clint began to lick Bonnie as Lily rode him up and down, leaving Darla out of it for the moment. The brunette acted immediately, though. She stretched out next to Clint, grabbed his left hand and placed it on her crotch. Feeling his way, he began to stoke her with his fingers until she was good and wet, and then she squealed when he inserted his middle finger into her.

He had to concentrate hard on what he was doing with his mouth, because Lily was increasing her tempo, riding his cock, and it was getting hard to think of anything else but what was building up inside of him. But it was Darla who went over the edge first, screaming as powerful tremors of pleasure spread through her

Lily was next, shouting out loud as her insides spasmed on Clint, yanking an explosion right out of him. And as he filled her with his seed, Bonnie suddenly stiffened, pressed herself tightly to his mouth and began to gush, wetting his face thoroughly.

The rest of the night went that way, and became a blur of breasts, butts, bodily fluids and hot, wet flesh . . .

Chapter Twenty-Eight

Clint woke the next morning with the 3 naked girls almost stacked up on him. The chair he had jammed under the doorknob was still there, and his gun was still within reach. But he needed to get off that bed, because he felt pinned down.

He managed to slide out from beneath all that beautiful flesh without waking the girls and got dressed. Grabbing his gun, he made his way back down the hall to his own room, where he washed and dressed for the day.

When he came downstairs, Taft was drinking coffee at the bar, and smiled at him.

"Nice night?"

"Entertaining," Clint said, "but far from restful. But do me a favor."

"What's that?"

"Don't send them to me again," Clint said.

"The girls will be hurt."

"They'll be fine," Clint said. "They'd probably prefer not to be told where, when and who to have sex with."

"Believe it or not," Taft said, "it was their idea. Lily's, actually."

"Still . . ."

"I get it," Taft said. "You like to pick your own ladies."

"That's it."

Taft leaned on the bar.

"But you had a good time, right?"

Clint grinned.

"What do you think?"

Taft laughed and stood up straight.

"Coffee? Breakfast?"

"You got anything else for me?"

Taft frowned.

"Well, not yet," the bartender said, "but I'm workin' it
over in my head—"

"I'll see you later, then."

"Don't wanna wait up for the girls?" Taft called after
him as he went out the front door.

***

Clint had not gotten what he needed from Taft, so he
decided he needed to go and see the sheriff, after all. As
he entered the office a young man with a badge on his
chest turned from the stove, holding a coffee pot. For a
moment Clint thought it might be the man who had
impersonated a deputy and sent him to be ambushed, but

it wasn't. For one thing, this one was older, and for another, the badge was too shiny and clean.

"Help ya, sir?" he asked.

"No thanks, Deputy," Clint said. "I was looking for the sheriff."

"Oh, he's havin' his breakfast just down the street. He should be back—"

"I'll go and see him there," Clint said.

"He don't like to be interrupted when he's eatin'," the man called after Clint.

"He'll talk to me," Clint called back, and went out the door.

***

Clint found Sheriff Hoskins sitting at a window table in a small restaurant about a block from his office.

"Don't you know sitting in the window is dangerous?" Clint asked, sitting across from the man.

"For you, maybe," Hoskins said. "For me it helps me watch the street, be on the lookout for trouble."

"You mean doing your job?"

Hoskins put a piece of ham into his mouth and chewed, then said, "I do my job, Adams."

"Okay, okay," Clint said. "I'm not here to ruin your breakfast."

"Then why are you here?"

"I need to ask you if you've seen someone."

"Not your guy again."

"No," Clint said, "the one who took a shot at me. I got his description from Weems."

"So it was Weems who treated his gunshot wound?"

"Yep."

"And he didn't tell you who it was?"

"He doesn't know," Clint said. "All he had was a description."

Clint told Hoskins what the man had looked like.

"And you believe 'im?"

"I do. Does he sound like somebody you've seen?"

"Well, sure."

"I mean, lately."

"I don't rightly remember," Hoskins said. "I mean, I've seen a few fellas who look like that."

"Well, give it some thought," Clint said. "If you think of one you've seen recently, let me know."

"Yeah, sure," Hoskins said. "Can I finish my breakfast now?"

Clint dropped some money onto the table.

"Be my guest," he said.

Chapter Twenty-Nine

Clint decided to go across to the Buffalo with his description to see if anyone there could help. As he entered he saw that there were 2 tables left, 5 men at each. Bat and Luke were at one table, while Anne's husband, Abel Terrell, was at the other. That meant there was a chance he would only have to face one of them, Bat or Luke.

He went to the bar, where Eddie was leaning on his elbows, watching the action. The blonde, Joi, was at the end of the bar, doing the same. There were no other girls in the place.

Eddie straightened when he saw Clint.

"Beer?"

"As long as it's not too early," Clint said.

"If it ain't too early for you, it ain't too early for me," Eddie said.

"Then I'll take it."

Eddie drew a beer and set it in front of Clint. Joi came down to join him.

"How's it going here?" he asked her.

"That one table is gonna come down to Bat and Luke," she said. "But everybody figured that."

"And the other one?"

"That man you're interested in, he's been havin' amazing luck."

"Sometimes that's all you need," Clint said.

"Well," Eddie said, "he's gonna need more than that to beat Bat Masterson or Luke Short."

"I don't know any of the other players," Clint said.

"Nobody does," Eddie said. "They ain't anybody—and they won't be, unless one of 'em wins this tournament."

Clint sipped his beer and set it down.

"I need to ask you both something," he said, and went on to describe the man who—according to Weems—had fired at him.

"Sounds like a lot of men," Joi said.

"A few I know of," Eddie said, "but I don't see why they'd shoot at you."

"Could just be because of who I am," Clint said. "Or they were sent after me. What about the phony deputy?" He described that young man, as well.

"You said your man Resnick has a big nose," Eddie said. "What these other men? The shooter? Anything like that?"

"Not that I know of. The phony deputy was just a fresh-faced young man."

"I've taken a lot of those up to my room," Joi said.

"And I've served beer to a lot of them," Eddie said.

"He may have just been a pawn," Clint said. "Not knowing what he was doing. But the one who pulled the trigger . . ."

"Tall, fair-haired, thirties," Eddie said. He looked at Joi. "Could be that fella from the Circle S."

"Jeffery?" She shook her head. "I don't think so."

"Why not?" Clint asked.

"I've spent some time with him," she said. "He's gentle, doesn't even wear a gun."

"That's true," Eddie said. "I've never seen him with a gun on his hip."

"All right, then," Clint said. "Who else?"

Eddie stroked his chin.

"Lemme give it some thought," he said.

"That's what I've been hearing," Clint said. "The sheriff, Taft, everybody's giving it some thought."

"There are a lot of people in town," Joi pointed out. "And living on the outskirts."

"Yeah, okay," Clint said, sourly. "If only somebody would spot that nose on Resnick's face."

"He must be in hidin'," Eddie said.

"That's for sure," Clint said, "but where?"

Eddie shrugged, and Joi went back to her end of the bar.

Clint turned and continued to watch the two tables.

Chapter Thirty

When it looked like the 2 tables were going to go on for some time—the chips simply moving around the table from player-to-player, with no one taking the advantage, yet—Clint thought he had to spend his time in a better way.

"I'll be back later," he told Eddie. "Keep thinking."

"I will."

When Joi commented that she had taken lots of fresh-faced young men to her room, it made him think. What about the girls at the Gold Rush? Bonnie, Darla and Lily might know something. They should have awakened and come downstairs by now.

When he entered the Gold Rush he saw the 3 girls at their table, eating. Lily waved and smiled.

"Back so soon?" Taft asked. "Have you eaten?"

"As a matter of fact, I haven't," Clint said. "I'll eat with the girls."

"Comin' up," Taft said.

He walked to their table and sat with them.

"Good morning, Clint," Bonnie said.

"Good morning."

"Did you sleep well?" Darla asked.

"I guess I did," he said. "I feel pretty good."

"You felt pretty good last night, too," Lily said, and the 3 girls laughed.

Taft brought over a plate of bacon and eggs and set it down in front of Clint, with a mug of coffee.

"Thanks."

"Sure thing."

He started eating, with all 3 of the girls watching him, while continuing to eat, themselves.

"Girls, I have a question to ask you," Clint said.

"The answer is yes," Lily said, "we all enjoyed ourselves last night."

"I did, too," he assured them, "but that wasn't the question. I want to describe a man, to see if any of you know who he is."

"All right," Darla said. "Go ahead."

He described the shooter, as Weems had described the man to him.

"Does that sound like anyone you know?" Clint asked. "Or anyone you've seen lately?"

The girls looked at each other.

"There've been a few men in and out of here like that," Lily said.

"Lately?" Clint asked.

"Whataya mean by lately?" Bonnie asked.

"The last few days."

"No," Darla said. "not that recently."

"Men of all sizes and shapes come in here, Clint," Lily said. "Unless there's somethin' else we can look for . . ."

"I don't have anything else," Clint said, "except that he was shot."

"So now you're lookin for two men?" Lily asked. "The one with the big nose, and this one, who was shot?"

"That's right."

"How did he get shot?" Darla asked.

"I shot him," Clint said, "when he tried to shoot me."

"Why'd he do that?" Lily asked.

"Maybe," Clint said, "because the one with the big nose sent him."

The 3 girls exchanged another look.

"We ain't seen anybody who's been shot," Darla said. "Not in the past few days."

"Okay," Clint said, chewing on a piece of bacon. "Thanks." He washed it down with some coffee.

"Are you bein' careful?" Lily asked. "I mean . . . we don't want you gettin' shot."

"I'm being real careful," Clint said.

At least, as careful as he could be without having somebody watch his back. He could have asked Bat or Luke for help, but they were in town to compete, and he didn't want to take them away from that.

And then he thought of somebody he knew he could trust.

"I've gotta go, girls," he said. "I'll see you later."

He stood up and headed for the door.

"Breakfast okay?" Taft asked.

"It was fine," Clint said, "there's just something I've got to do."

***

When he knocked on Anne Archer's door she opened it and looked surprised.

"Breakfast again?" she asked. "I've already—"

"No," Clint said, "not that. Didn't you say you've still got your gun?"

"Yes," she said, "it's in my trunk. But what—"

"Tell me, how would you feel about strapping it on again?" he asked.

She looked confused.

"What for?"

"Maybe," he said, "to keep me alive."

Chapter Thirty-One

Clint watched as Anne walked to her trunk, opened it and retrieved her gunbelt.

"When was the last time you wore it?" he asked.

"I don't know, months?" she said, unfurling it and setting it on the bed. She removed the gun from the holster, checked it and returned it.

"What did you mean by keepin' you alive?" she asked.

"I need somebody to watch my back."

"How about Bat, or Luke Short?"

"They're a little busy, right now," Clint said. "I don't want to take them away from their tables."

"Don't you think they'd do it?"

"Oh, they'd walk away in a minute to watch my back," Clint assured her. "I'm just not going to ask them to do it."

"But you'll ask me?"

"It'll get you out of this room."

"Good point." She looked down at herself, and the dress she was wearing, and spread her arms. "Well, I can't work in this."

"Don't tell me you don't have any trousers."

"I do," she said, "but I haven't worn them in a while, either. Abel likes me in dresses."

"Guess I can't blame him for that."

"I'll just change."

She walked to the trunk and fished out a pair of trousers, and a plaid shirt, then turned and looked at him, holding them in her arms.

"Are you gonna watch me change?" she asked, with a smile, "Because if you are, we ain't gonna get out of this room any time soon."

He knew she was right. Once she started undressing, all bets would be off.

"I'll, uh, just wait out in the hall."

She stared at him for a moment, then said, "That might be a good idea."

He nodded, backed toward the door, groped for the knob and then stepped out of the room, closing the door behind him. Then he stood there and tried not to imagine what was going on inside.

After a few moments he stepped away from the door and leaned against the opposing wall. When the door opened the Anne Archer he knew stepped out, trousers, boots and shirt, the gun strapped to her waist.

"What's next?" she asked.

"I've been looking for two men," he said. "So we're going to keep looking."

***

Out on the street Clint and Anne Archer drew looks while walking side-by-side. With her there to watch his back, he didn't feel so much like there was a bullseye painted there. Hopefully, whoever wanted him killed would try a more frontal approach.

"Well, well," Clint heard a man's voice say.

They both turned and saw Sheriff Hoskins crossing the street to them.

"Miss Archer," he said. "I thought you put this part of your life in the past when you married Abel."

"Clint needs somebody to watch his back," she said. "Obviously, he can't trust it to you."

"Wait a minute," Clint said to Hoskins, "you know Abel Terrell?"

"Yeah," Hoskins said, "we're friends. So what?"

Clint looked at Anne.

"I thought you knew," she said.

"No, I didn't."

"What's the difference?" Hoskins asked. "I knew about you two."

"How did you know that?" Anne asked.

"Abel told me," Hoskins said. "I gotta get on with my rounds. You two try not to kill anybody."

They both watched the sheriff walk away, then Clint turned to Anne.

"I thought you and Abel rode into this town for the poker game," he said.

"We did."

"You didn't get married here? Live here?"

"No," she said. "We got married in St. Louis, and we live in a house in St. Joe."

"When you came all the way here for this, Abel found his friend Hoskins was the sheriff?"

"That's the way it happened," she said. "Coincidence."

Clint made a face.

"Oh, I know how you feel about coincidences," she said, "but this was one."

"Okay," he said. "Let's go to some of the restaurants in town."

"You hungry already?"

"No," he said, "but maybe a waiter or waitress will recognize one of the men I'm looking for from their descriptions."

Chapter Thirty-Two

The problem was the same.

Resnick's nose would make him stand out, but nobody had seen a man like that.

The shooter had nothing about him that would make him stand out. All the waiters and waitresses they spoke to had seen men like that.

In the last place they went they got a table and had lunch.

"What's next?" she asked.

"I might have to talk to Weems again," Clint said. "There's got to be something about the shooter that people can notice."

"Like the fact that he's been shot?" she asked. "Is he wearing a sling?"

"I don't know," Clint said. "Weems treated his shoulder. He could be bandaged and wearing a shirt over it."

"Then he'd be movin' stiffly."

"Maybe."

"And maybe once he was bandaged he left town," she offered. "I mean, since he missed you, whoever sent him wouldn't want him to be seen."

"Good point."

"And if they sent somebody after you once, they'll probably do it again."

"Another good point."

"And points you've already thought of."

"Yes."

"Which is why you need me to watch your back."

"Exactly."

"So what do we do?" she asked. "Just walk around until they make another try?"

"Maybe we should split up," Clint said.

"But I thought—"

"You could still watch my back," he said, "but not so obviously. After all, they might not make another try while we're together."

"But if they think you're alone . . . I get it."

"So I'll leave here by myself when we're done, and you follow," Clint said.

"You think they'll buy that?"

"I don't know," Clint said, "but I guess we'll find out."

***

"When are you gonna get rid of Adams?" Resnick asked. "I need to move on."

"We already tried it once," the man said. "My man got shot."

"I'm payin' you enough," Resnick said. "Get him fixed up and send somebody else."

"I've got two men coming in to do the job," the other man said. "They should be here soon."

"And your first shooter?" Resnick asked. "What if Adams spots him?"

"He's gone," the man said, "Left town. I didn't want Adams to find him."

Resnick looked around the shack he was staying in. It was dark and depressing.

"Don't you have someplace better I can stay?" he demanded. "Someplace . . . brighter."

"You need to stay out of sight," the man said. "Like you said, you're paying me, so do as I say and the job will get done."

"It better!" Resnick said.

The man moved to the door.

"Hey," Resnick called out, "what about somethin' to eat? I'm starvin'."

"It's on the way."

"And have a girl bring it," Resnick said. "And tell her to stay a while."

"That'll be up to her," the man said.

"Don't they do what you tell 'em?"

"They do what I pay them to do," the man answered, "their jobs. So if you pay her enough . . ."

"I get it," Resnick said.

"Good," the man said, and left.

***

Clint and Anne Archer finished their lunch and he paid the bill.

"I'm thinking about something you said a little while ago," Clint said.

"What's that?"

"That the shooter probably left town," Clint said. "I thought about that, but I never acted on it."

"So you're gonna check the livery stables?"

"Exactly," Clint said. "If he did ride out, he needed a horse."

"Well," she replied, "like we said, you go first and I'll follow."

"Try not to be noticed," he said. "I know that'll be hard, since you're so beautiful."

"Flattery," she said, "will get you everywhere."

Chapter Thirty-Three

Clint had checked all the livery stables in town for Resnick, so he knew where they were. He started with the one he had left Eclipse in.

"You haven't come for him, have you?" the hostler asked. "I haven't had a horse like him, in . . . well, ever."

"No, I'm not leaving town yet," Clint assured the man. "But I'm looking for someone who may have." He described the shooter to the man.

"Lots of fellas like that have come through here, but none in the last few days," he said. "Sorry."

"That's okay," Clint said. "I just wanted to check here first. I'll try the others."

"Try Quate."

"Who's Quate?"

"Lives at the north end of town. He has some horses. Anybody who wants to get out of town without bein' seen usually buys a horse from him."

"Will he talk to me?"

"Tell him Clarence sent you. He'll talk to ya."

"Thanks, Clarence."

"Anythin' I can do to keep that horse of yours here a little longer," Clarence said, with a toothless smile.

***

Clint had to give Anne Archer credit. She managed to follow him from the livery to the north end of town, with him just barely seeing her. He knew, to others, she would go unseen.

When the got to the north end he found a small compound with a dilapidated house, a newly renovated barn, and a corral with about half a dozen horses in it. Apparently, this fellow Quate took better care of his horses than he did of himself.

As Clint approached on foot, a large man with long hair, sloping shoulders, and a bow-legged gate came out of the barn.

"Whataya want?" the man demanded. His arms, though not defined with muscle, were very thick. Clint knew this was the kind of man who was strong enough to lift and move anvils at his leisure.

"My name's Clint Adams. Clarence told me to come and see you."

"You know Clarence?"

"He's taking care of my horse."

"You're the Gunsmith."

"That's right."

"That means your horse is a Darley Arabian."

"Right again."

"I'd like to see that animal."

"Be my guest," Clint said. "Clarence has him now."

Quate looked Clint up and down, then waved with his right hand and said, "Come on in."

The big man turned and walked away, so Clint followed him into the barn. There were other horses in stalls, and one standing in the center of the barn. Apparently, Quate had been shoeing him when he heard Clint come walking up. The man must have excellent hearing.

"You mind if I keep workin'?" Quate asked.

"Not at all."

Quate bent to lift the horse's left front leg. He scraped out some mud that had caked there, then set the horseshoe in place and started to nail it.

"What can I do for you?"

"I'm looking for a man who may have left town," Clint said. "But he wouldn't have wanted to be seen. Clarence said that men like that sometimes buy horses from you."

Quate didn't reply until he had finished affixing the shoe to the horse's hoof. He set his tools down and turned to face Clint.

"I sold three horses this week," he said. "What's your man look like?"

"Tall, fair-haired, in his thirties, with a bullet wound in his shoulder."

"Oh yeah," Quate said. "I remember him."

"You do?"

Quate nodded.

"He left yesterday," Quate said. "Paid me twice what I asked for."

"What was his name?"

"We didn't get into that," Quate said. "That's the way it is in a lot of cases."

"Money talks."

Quate nodded.

"That's it."

"Did he say anything else?" Clint asked. "Anybody's name?"

"He said Bart, at one point."

"Bart?" Clint asked. "Bart who?"

"It sounded like part of a name," Quate said. "He stopped himself before he said the full name."

"Quate, how much do you know about town?"

"I know Clarence," he said. "And I go to the general store for my supplies. That's about it."

"Why is that?"

"I don't like people," Quate said.

"I can't say I blame you," Clint said. "There are a lot of people I don't like, either."

"I can deal with Clarence," Quate said. "And I force myself to go to the general store. And I can deal with somebody like you. But most people just . . . disgust me."

"Yet you sell them horses?"

Quate shrugged his sloping shoulders.

"A man's gotta make a livin'." He put his hand on the animal he had just shoed. "Besides, I like horses, and they like me."

Clint was surprised that the animal seemed to be leaning into the big man's touch.

"All right," Clint said. "Thanks for the information."

"Are you going after him?" Quate said. "He rode out to the north, but I don't know where he was headed."

"No," Clint said, "he can go. He was sent after me, and I want the man who sent him."

"This Bart?"

"Yes."

"And do you know who he is?"

"I have a good idea," Clint said.

Chapter Thirty-Four

"Bartlett?" Anne Archer asked.

"That's the only Bart I can think of," Clint told her.

Anne had watched as he approached Quate's compound and had been waiting when he left it.

"Are you gonna accuse him?"

"Not yet," Clint said. "There just might be somebody else in town named Bart."

"Then let's get back and find out," she said. "Should I keep following you?"

"Yes," Clint said. "just in case."

"Right."

He moved ahead of her. She waited several moments, then began to follow.

***

Clint decided to go to the Gold Rush and talk to Taft. He was the one person Clint felt he could trust.

"Bart?" Taft asked. "Could mean Bartlett."

"That's what I thought," Clint said, "that the man started to say Bartlett and cut himself off. But is there anyone else in town named Bart? Maybe a first name?"

"Well," Taft said, "I wasn't much help with your shooter, but this . . . if there was a man named Bart in town, I'd probably know about it."

"What about the girls?" Clint said.

"We can ask 'em," Taft said. "They're upstairs dressing. They'll be down in a while. Have a beer."

"Why not?"

Clint felt bad about having a beer while Anne had to stand outside and watch, but it tasted too good for him to feel guilty for very long.

He was halfway through the mug when Bonnie came down, first.

"Clint," she said, joining him at the bar. She was wearing a green dress that showed off the upper slopes of her large breasts.

"You look beautiful," he said.

"Thank you. What brings you back so soon?" she asked, giving him an arched eyebrow. "I hope it's me."

"Can I tell you a secret?" he asked.

"Please do."

"If I was going to come back here for one of you," he said. "It would be you."

She put both her hands on his arm.

"I was hoping you'd say that."

"But I'm actually back here just to ask a question," he told her.

"More questions?" She moved her hands. "Go ahead."

"Do you know a man named Bart?"

"Bart who?"

"I don't know," Clint said. "Bart something, or something Bart. I don't even know if it's a first or last name. But apparently he sent the man who took a shot at me."

She thought a moment, then said, "The only name that comes to mind right now is Bartlett. Could that be it? Big Bill Bartlett sent somebody to kill you?"

"It's starting to look that way," Clint said.

"But why?"

"Guess I'm going to have to ask him."

At that moment Lily and Darla came down, one dressed in red and the other in blue. He asked them the same question, and neither of them knew a man named Bart.

"But all the men we take upstairs," Lily pointed out, "don't always tell us their names."

"I realize that," Clint said, "but I'm going to have to go with the only name that comes to mind."

"Big Bill," Taft said.

Chapter Thirty-Five

Clint had no choice but to go across the street to the Buffalo and confront Big Bill Bartlett. As he entered he saw that the game had finally come down to one table. Both Bat and Luke were there, with Abel Terrell and 2 other players he didn't know.

"Just in time," Eddie said, when Clint reached the bar. "They're just startin' the final table."

"Interesting," Clint said, "but I'm looking for Big Bill. Is he around?"

"I just sent Joi to get 'im," Eddie said. "He wanted to watch the final table. Should be here in a minute or two. Can I get you somethin'?"

"Beer," Clint said.

"Comin' up."

As Eddie set it down in front of him, Clint said, "I never asked, Eddie, what does this game do for security? Other than the two men on the front door?"

"There are a couple of other men," Eddie said. "They can see you, but you can't see them."

Clint looked around and spotted what he hadn't noticed before, slits in the walls on either side. No gun barrels showing, but he was sure they were there.

"I see."

If Big Bill Bartlett wanted him dead, they could have shot him any time. But perhaps Bartlett didn't want it done inside his own saloon.

"Here comes the boss," Eddie said.

Clint turned, saw Bartlett walking across the floor with Joi. The other tables had been pushed aside, with chairs stacked on them, so that there was plenty of room around the final table.

Bartlett reached the bar and joined Clint, while Joi took up her position at the other end.

"Mr. Adams," Bartlett said, "have you come to watch the final table?"

"Not really," Clint said, "but I'd like to bring in a guest to watch it."

"Of course," Bartlett said, "anyone you want."

"Thanks, I'll go and get her."

Clint walked to the batwing doors and stepped out. Anne Archer joined him.

"Time to come inside and watch your husband at work," Clint said.

"The final table?"

"Yes. But I also need you to watch the gun slits in two walls."

"I understand."

"Okay, then let's go in."

They entered the Buffalo and walked to the bar, where Bartlett was still standing, holding a beer.

"And who's this lovely lady?" he asked.

"My name," Anne said, "is Anne Terrell."

It was odd for Clint to hear her say her married name. He had never thought of her that way.

"Terrell?" Bartlett repeated. "Abel's wife?"

"That's right."

At that moment Abel Terrell looked over and saw her.

"Anne!"

He stood up from the table and walked over, frowning at his wife.

"What're you doin' here? And why are you dressed like that and wearin' a gun?"

"I'm helpin' Clint, Abel."

"So, your old boyfriend has you wearin' a gun again?" he demanded. Looking at Clint he snapped, "I told you to stay away from my wife."

"You just told me to remember she's your wife, and I do," Clint said.

"What the hell are you doin'—" Terrell started.

"I'm watching Clint's back," she said. "Somebody tried to kill him."

"That's his business!" Terrell snapped. "Why doesn't he get one of his friends to watch his back."

"Because," Clint said, "they're busy taking your money."

"You think so?"

There was the sound of chairs being pushed back and then Clint saw Bat and Luke were standing. The game had come to a halt as they approached the bar.

"What's goin' on?" Bat asked. "What's this about somebody tryin' to kill you?"

"Took a shot at me," Clint said. "They tried to ambush me."

"Who was it?" Luke asked.

"I don't know," Clint said. "The shooter was sent after me by someone. I wounded him and he left town."

"So who sent him?" Bat asked. "And why didn't you come to us?"

"You fellas are a little busy," Clint said, "so I asked Anne to watch my back. She agreed."

"Is this about Resnick, the man you were trailin'?" Bat asked.

"I don't know," Clint said. "I'd have to ask whoever sent the shooter after me."

"And you don't know who that was," Luke said.

"No," Clint said, "not for sure."

"What's that mean?" Bat asked.

"I have a name," Clint said, "or part of a name."

"What is it," Bat asked.

"Yes," Bartlett said, "what's the name?"

Clint looked at Bartlett.

"That's what I came here to talk to you about, Big Bill," Clint said.

"Why me?"

"Because," Clint said, "the name I have is Bart."

"Bart," Big Bill said. "What does that have to do with me?"

"It's part of your name," Clint said. "The shooter was saying a name, and stopped short."

"And who told you this?"

"A fella named Quate."

"That crazy—so Quate tells you about this 'Bart' and you believe him?" Big Bill asked.

"I do," Clint said. "And now I'm asking you, did you send someone to ambush me?"

They all stared at Big Bill Bartlett, waiting for his answer.

Chapter Thirty-Six

"No."

"Just no?" Clint asked.

"What else would you want me to say?"

Clint looked around. Maybe there were too many people listening.

"Why don't you all go back to your game?" Clint suggested.

"That sounds like a good idea," Big Bill Bartlett said. The smallest man in the room, he had to look up at all of them. "There's still money to be won."

"Yeah," one of the men still at the table called out, "can we get back to it?"

Bat looked at Clint.

"If you need help you know where to find us."

"I know," Clint said.

"No matter what?" Luke added.

"Thanks."

They turned to go back to the game, but Bat stopped and looked back.

"You comin', Terrell?"

"I'm comin'," Terrell said, sourly. He looked at his wife. "You go back to the hotel."

"I will after we find out who tried to shoot Clint."

"Damn it, Anne—"

"You better get back to your game," she said, cutting him off. "That's why we're here, isn't it?"

Terrell scowled, gave Clint a hard look, and then walked back to the table, where the other 4 players were waiting for him.

"Okay," Clint said to Big Bill, "how about now?"

"I still didn't send anybody to shoot you," Bartlett said. "Hell, if I wanted you dead, I could have you shot right here."

"Huh-uh," Clint said. "Too many witnesses."

"Why the hell would I want you dead?" Bartlett asked.

"His reputation?" Anne answered.

"Means nothin' to me," Bartlett said. "I'm more impressed with Bat Masterson and Luke Short."

"You know anybody else in town named Bart?" Clint asked.

"No."

"First name? Last name? Nickname?"

Bartlett hesitated.

"What are you thinking?" Clint asked.

"I don't want to point at someone else just to get you off my back."

"But?"

"Well, there's a fella I know, his name's Burt Simms."

"Burt?"

"Could your man have said Burt, not Bart?"

"I don't know," Clint said. "I'll have to check. Where do I find Burt Simms?"

"He has a ranch outside of town," Big Bill said. "He and his men come in here, sometimes."

Clint looked at Eddie, who shrugged.

"It never occurred to me," the bartender said. "Besides, I think of him as Mr. Simms, and his men always just call 'im 'Boss.'"

Clint looked at Anne.

"You up for a ride?"

"Sure," she said.

"Maybe you want to stay here and watch the game?" Clint asked. That had been his plan, to have her watch her husband lose and see the effect, but now things were changing.

"No," she said, "I'll go along with you. According to you he's gonna lose. Do I wanna see that?"

"He's been real lucky up to now," Big Bill pointed out.

"Yeah," she said, "up to now, but how long can that last?"

"Well," Big Bill said, "considering who else is at that table, not long."

She looked at Clint.

"Ready?"

Chapter Thirty-Seven

They went to the livery where Clint had left Eclipse and rented a horse for Anne from Clarence.

"Did you see Quate?" Clarence asked.

"I saw him," Clint said. "Thanks. He gave me something to think about. He's an odd one.

Clarence nodded.

"Yeah, real odd. But he's okay."

"I'll take your word for it," Clint said.

Clint and Anne walked their horses outside, then mounted up and rode out following the directions they had been given to reach Burt Simms' ranch.

***

After Clint and Anne left the Buffalo, Big Bill said to Eddie, "Keep an eye on the game. I'll be back."

"Right, boss."

As he passed Joi she asked, "Do you want me to come with you?"

"No," he said. "Stay here and do your job."

"Yes, boss," she said, trying to hide the hurt she felt. His tone had been a cold one, which she wasn't used to.

As he entered his office she walked down to Eddie and asked, "What's goin' on, I thought he wanted to watch the final table?"

"He did," Eddie said.

"Then what's changed his mind?"

"I don't know."

"Damn it!" someone yelled from the table.

Eddie and Joi watched one of the players stand up and storm off, out of the saloon.

"We're down to four," Eddie said.

"Should I tell the boss?"

"No, he said he'd be back. Let's just . . . wait."

***

"There it is," Clint said, looking at the house in the distance. Across from it was a barn and corral. "Come on."

They rode through a wooden entry arch, beneath a sign that said CIRCLE S RANCH, and approached the house. There were 4 men in the corral who stopped to look at them.

Clint and Anne dismounted, went up 5 steps to a porch and approached the front door of the house. Clint knocked and waited. Over at the corral, the 4 men had gone back to work.

The door was opened by a middle-aged woman with greying black hair.

"Yes? Can I help you?"

"I'm here to see Mr. Simms," Clint said.

"What—who are you?" the woman asked.

"My name's Clint Adams, and this is Anne Archer," Clint said. "We've ridden here from town to talk to Mr. Simms. Is he here?"

"Clint Adams?"

"That's right."

Anne stood next to Clint, not bothering to correct his usage of her maiden name.

"If you'll wait here I'll ask Mr. Simms if he'll see you," the woman said.

"Thank you."

She withdrew and closed the door.

"Terrell," she said.

"What?" He looked at her.

"My name is Anne Terrell."

"Sorry," he said, "I just can't think of you that way."

"It probably doesn't matter," she said. "I don't think my name will be Terrell much longer."

"Maybe after the game is over—"

"No," she said, "the marriage was a mistake from the start. Asking you for your help was just my way of keeping you from leavin' town. Seein' you has convinced me I don't want to be married to Abel any longer."

"Maybe that'll change."

"I doubt it."

"Then I'm sorr—" he started, but the door opened, cutting him off, and the woman reappeared.

"Mr. Simms will see you," she said. "He's in the living room. Follow me."

She turned and went into the house. They followed, with Anne closing the front door behind them.

Burt Simms was a large man in his 60s, wearing work clothes, a rancher who was hands on.

"Mr. Adams," he said, as they followed the woman in, "you and the lady are welcome. Thank you, Maya."

The woman nodded and left.

"Maya's my housekeeper," Simms said. "Can I get you somethin' to drink?"

"No, thanks," Clint said.

"Then why don't you tell me what I can do for the Gunsmith?" Simms asked.

"I'm looking for a man who tried to bushwhack me," Clint said. "I managed to shoot him but he got away."

"Why are you here lookin' for him?"

"He bought a horse from a man named Quate."

"I know Quate," Simms said, "but that still doesn't explain—"

"He said the name 'Bart' or 'Burt' to Quate before he left town."

"Ah," Simms said. "You think I sent him to kill you, for some reason?"

"I'm just asking questions," Clint said.

"Describe this man to me."

Clint did, and he could see that Simms recognized him.

"I had a man named Collins working for me," he admitted. "He's gone missing. Maybe now I know why."

"Why would he try to kill me?" Clint asked.

"I don't know," Simms said, "but maybe my foreman can shed some light. I'll send Maya for him. Excuse me."

Simms left the room. Anne looked at Clint.

"What if he comes back with five or six guns?" she asked.

"I guess we'll have to be ready for that."

They drew their guns from their holsters, checked them, and slid them back.

Chapter Thirty-Eight

Simms came back alone, and Clint and Anne relaxed.

The man looked at both of them and asked, "Did you think I was coming back with a gang of gunmen?"

"We were ready," Clint said.

"Can't say that I blame you, with the kind of life you've lived," Simms said. "But let me assure you, I have no reason for wanting you dead."

"That's what I came here to find out."

"So if it's not 'Burt' it's 'Bart'?" Simms asked. "As in Big Bill Bartlett?"

"That's how we're thinking," Clint said. "We spoke with him, then decided to come and see you."

"Does he know you came out here?"

"He does."

"Then if I was you, I'd watch myself on the ride back," Simms suggested.

"We intend to," Clint said, "but if someone tries to bushwhack us, it could still be him, or you."

"Well," Simms said, "here's my foreman. Let's see what he has to say."

A man in his 40s entered the room, sweating, his shirt sleeves rolled up to reveal powerful forearms. He wasn't wearing a gun, or a hat.

"Maya said you wanted to see me, boss," he said, stealing a look at Anne.

"Nick," Simms said, "Meet Clint Adams, and his lady friend—"

"This is Anne Terrell," Clint said. "She's an experienced bounty hunter."

"Ah . . ." Simms said. "I'm sorry, Miss Terrell."

"It's Mrs.," she said, "and it's okay."

"Adams?" the foreman asked. "The Gunsmith?"

"That's right," Simms said. "Adams, this is Nick Tate, my foreman for ten years, now."

Tate came across the floor to shake hands with Clint, and then nodded toward Anne.

"What's this about, boss?" Tate asked.

"Adams is looking for a man who used to work here."

"Used to?" Tate asked.

"Yes, he's missing in action," Simms said.

"Oh, you mean Harlan?"

"That's his name," Simms said, looking at Clint. "Harlan Kelly."

"Where is he?" Tate asked Clint.

"He left town," Clint said, "right after he took a shot at me."

"What?"

"I put a bullet in him, instead," Clint said. "He got patched up by a man named Weems, bought a horse from a man named Quate, and then left town."

"And you wanna find him?" Tate asked.

"No," Clint said, "I want to find the man who sent him after me."

"And you think he got sent from here?" Tate asked. "No way."

"Then why did he do it?" Clint asked. "Was he the kind of man who's after a reputation?"

"Not that I could see," Tate said. "But he was the kind of man who complained."

"About what?" Anne asked.

"About not havin' enough money," Tate said. "So if somebody offered him a lot of money, that might have made him take a shot at you."

"Okay," Clint said, "but who offered him the money?"

"Did he have any friends here who might know?" Anne asked.

"No," Tate said.

"No friends?" Clint asked.

"He didn't make friends," Tate said. "He wasn't likeable. The truth is, if he hadn't disappeared I probably would've fired him."

Chapter Thirty-Nine

As Clint and Anne rode back to town they discussed the situation.

"What did that accomplish?" she asked.

"I believed them," Clint said, simply. "They didn't send Harlan Kelly after me."

"Then who did?"

"Our only choice is Big Bill Bartlett."

"But why?" Anne asked. "And why don't you believe him? And one more thing. Don't you think if Big Bill wanted you dead, he could send somebody better than a disgruntled ranch hand like Kelly?"

"You'd think so," Clint said, "but maybe he wasn't being paid enough."

"So you think somebody was payin' him to pay Kelly? And who would that be?" she asked. "The man you were lookin' for in the first place?"

"Right," Clint said. "And that means we're back to Harry Resnick."

***

As soon as Clint and Anne left to ride out to the Circle S, Big Bill Bartlett entered the shed behind the Buffalo Saloon.

"Finally!" Harry Resnick said. "You wanna tell me what the hell is goin' on?"

"You're going to have to go deeper into your pockets if you want me to get rid of the Gunsmith," Bartlett told him.

"Whataya talkin' about?"

"He just came into my place and asked me if I sent someone to kill him."

"What'd you tell 'im?"

"What do you think I told him?" Bartlett asked.

"Where is he now?"

"I sent him on a wild goose chase," Bartlett said. "But if you want him taken care of, it'll have to be now, so let's see the money, Resnick."

"You've got money," Resnick grumbled. "You've got plenty of it."

"That's my money," Bartlett said. "This is your problem and taking care of it has to be done with your money. So let's see it."

Grumbling, Resnick stood up and reached over for his saddlebags.

***

As Burt Simms had needlessly suggested, Clint and Anne were on the lookout for an ambush on their way back to town.

They each scanned the horizon ahead, and behind them, as well as either side of them. But in the end there was only 2 sets of eyes, and too many directions. When the shots came, they were not surprised. There was high ground surrounding them, so there was no way of telling where they were coming from.

They both vaulted off their horses to the ground, landing hard, but rolling to diminish the impact, somewhat. Shots continued to ring out, and lead chewed up the ground around them as they scrambled for cover.

"So?" Anne asked. "Whataya think now?"

"Simms didn't have enough time to set this up," Clint said. "Big Bill did."

"Okay," Anne said, "so Resnick's payin' Big Bill to get rid of you for him."

"Looks like it," Clint said. "Now we just have to get out of this predicament."

"I still have one question," Anne said.

"What's that?"

"Why would Big Bill bother with this, when he's got that poker tournament going on?"

"I think Big Bill," Clint said, "might just be trying to prove how big he really is."

***

The shooters stared down at Clint and Anne Archer as they scrambled for cover.

"Should we stop firing?" Frank Harris asked.

"No," his boss, Alan Koenig replied. "Just keep firin' a little longer, to give them somethin' to think about."

The 2 men across the way from them would keep firing as long as they did.

Harris and Koenig fired until their rifles were empty, then stopped. Beamish and Lane also stopped.

"Okay," Koenig said, "just reload."

"Are we supposed to kill the woman?" Harris asked, while obeying.

"She's with him," Koenig said. "Whatever happens to her happens."

Once they reloaded they pointed the rifles down at where Clint and Anne had taken cover.

"Should we go down after them?" Harris asked.

"Let's just wait a few minutes and see what they do," Koenig said. "Don't fire unless I do."

"Right."

They watched, and waited.

Below, Clint and Anne were doing the same thing.

"How many do you figure?" Anne asked.

"At least four," Clint said, pointing. "Two there, two there. They have rifles."

Anne noticed that Clint had grabbed his rifle before leaping from Eclipse's back. She hadn't had the same presence of mind.

"I should have my rifle," she said. "I've been away from this for too long."

"Here, take mine."

"No, I—"

"Take it! I can do damage with my pistol."

"Yeah, you can," Anne said, accepting the rifle. "You can do anything with your guns. Why would I forget that?"

"You haven't," Clint said, grabbing his gun from his holster. "You just needed reminding."

"So what do we do now?" she asked.

"You think you can handle two of them?" he asked.

"I can do it," she said. "Like you said, I just needed reminding."

"Okay, then," Clint said, pointing, "you take the two up there, and I'll take the two over there."

"Let's move!" she said.

Chapter Forty

Clint and Anne both broke from cover and ran in opposite directions. They could hear bullets striking the ground right behind them as the shooters opened fire.

They both started to work their way up their slopes from the side, the men on top scrambling to change their positions.

There was more cover on the slopes than there had been on flat ground, and Clint and Anne were both using it effectively to work their way up, despite the fact that they were still being fired on.

But, worried about each other as they were, they had to tend to their own business.

***

Clint made his way up the slope, going from rock to tree to rock while the men at the top fired at him. He had his gun in his hand, but he didn't bother with a shot until he had a clear line of sight to a target.

***

"What the hell is he doin'?" Harris asked. "He's crazy. He's runnin' right at us."

"Yeah, well," Koenig said, "maybe we oughtta let him reach us."

"What?" Harris fired again.

"Hold your fire until he gets closer," Koenig said.

"Are you crazy?" Harris asked. "That's the Gunsmith."

"Yeah," Koenig said, "that's why we're gettin' paid what we're gettin' paid."

"You ain't told me what we're gettin' paid," Harris said.

"I will," Koenig said, "after the job's done."

Harris looked down the hill.

"He's still comin'," he said.

"Wait," Koenig said.

***

On the other side Beamish and Lane were having much the same problem, and conversation.

"She's still comin'," Beamish said.

"And we still gotta kill 'er," Lane said, "so keep firin'."

***

166

Anne Archer Terrell saw the 2 men at the top of the hill, firing down at her, but since she was zig-zagging her way up the slope, they weren't coming close to hitting her. Apparently, they didn't realize that all they had to do was wait until she got closer, but she had to do something before that thought occurred to them.

So she stopped running, raised Clint's rifle, and sighted along the barrel.

***

Clint kept working his way up the slope, aware that the 2 men had stopped shooting at him. From across the way he still heard shots, but that was for Anne Archer to deal with, at the moment.

He knew what was going on ahead of him. They had backed away from the edge, so that they couldn't see him and he couldn't see them, anymore. But he knew they were waiting for him to get closer.

Which he wasn't going to do.

So he stopped running.

***

Anne's first shot took Beamish right in the chest, as he was leaning over to get a clear shot at her.

Lane saw her stop running and raise her rifle and thought it might be a good idea to get out of sight, so he stepped back. When the bullet spun Beamish around, Lane caught sight of the dead look in his friend's eyes before he fell onto his face.

Lane turned and started running.

***

"Now what's he doin'?" Harris demanded.

He and Koenig had stepped back to wait, so they couldn't see Clint. They simply assumed he would keep running until he reached the top. And when he came up over the lips of the hill, they were going to gun him down.

Only he didn't show.

"What the—" Koenig said. "Harris, take a look and see what he's doin'."

"What?" Harris asked. "Why me?"

"Because I'm in charge here," Koenig said.

"We're all gettin' paid—"

"But I'm the only one who knows how much, remember?" Koenig asked. "And I'm the one who's gonna collect the money when the job's done. And you ain't gettin' paid unless you look over that ledge there and kill the Gunsmith."

"Damn you, Koenig."

Harris inched toward the edge, peered over and immediately fell back at Koenig's feet with a bullet in his forehead.

Chapter Forty-One

Clint moved closer to the top, now convinced he was dealing with a single shooter.

"Can you hear me up there?" he called out. He wondered if the man could get to his horse?

"I hear ya," a man's voice said.

"It's kind of quiet now," Clint said. "I think the shooting across the way is finished. There might only be you and me left."

"Or your lady friend is dead and the rest of my men are on their way over here."

"Oh, I think that's wishful thinking on your part," Clint said. "I'm pretty sure it's just you and me."

After a moment of silence, the man's voice asked, "So how do you wanna do this?"

"Well, I could come up there and we could do it face-to-face," Clint said, "but since you just tried to ambush me, I don't think that's an option, is it?"

"I'm gonna blow your head off the minute you show it," the man said.

"That's what I thought."

"So come on up, Adams," the man invited.

"I think I will," Clint said.

He looked across the way at the hill Anne had attacked. It was still quiet, and he preferred to think Anne had come out on top of that encounter. So that left him and this fellow. He could wait for Anne to show up, or he could just go up and get it over with.

"I'm going to give you a chance to walk away from this," Clint said. "Drop your gun and tell me who sent you? Then you can go."

"You think I'm afraid of your reputation?" the man asked.

"If you're not," Clint said, "you should be."

"Come on, Adams!" the man shouted. "Let's get it over with."

Clint knew he couldn't just walk up over the edge. He'd be walking into a bullet. He looked to his left and right. The hill was too steep on the left, but he saw that he could move a few feet to the right, where there were some rocks he could use for good footing.

"Adams!"

The man sounded nervous, which was good. Clint knew he would be looking from right to left, to see at what point Clint was going to appear.

He moved to his right, got himself situated with his feet planted, then bent his knees before springing up over the top, tumbling forward, coming up on one knee with his gun extended. The man there was surprised. He fired first, but the shot was off the mark. Clint's shot wasn't.

The man folded in half and went down. Clint hurried to him, hoping to find him alive so he could question him. But, when he turned the man over, he was dead.

"Damn!" he swore.

He went to the other man, but he knew his bullet had caught that one in the forehead. There was no way he was alive, and he was right.

He took a moment to replace his spent shell before holstering his gun and starting down the hill.

***

At the bottom he found Anne Archer—that was still the way he thought of her—standing there with an unhappy looking man.

"This is my friend Lane," Anne said. "He was tryin' to get away, but as you can see, he didn't make it."

"I had two up there," Clint said. "They're both dead."

"I had two," she said, "but Lane didn't make me kill him. He was smart enough to give up."

"Okay, Lane," Clint said. "Do you know who I am?"

"I know," Lane, a young man, said. "You're the Gunsmith."

"Who was the leader of this little ambush party?" Clint asked.

"That was Koenig," he said. "I guess you killed him."

"Big fellow, big mouth?"

"That was him."

"Yep, he's dead. Who was the other one?"

"Harris," Lane said. "I didn't know him. We just met."

"And who was with you?"

"Beamish. He knew Koenig and got me the job."

"The job of killing two people," Clint said.

Lane looked away.

"We was gonna get paid a lot of money."

"Now here's the big question," Clint said. "By who? Who was footing the bill?"

"Koenig was the only one who knew that," Lane said. "I swear."

Lane looked scared, so Clint believed him.

"Where are your horses?" he asked.

"We left them a ways away so they wouldn't be heard," Lane said.

"Well, let's go and get them," Clint said. "We're going back to town, where you're going to meet the sheriff."

"Do I hafta?"

"Would you rather be dead?"

"No," the young man muttered.

Clint looked at Anne and said, "Let's get our horses."

Chapter Forty-Two

Rounding up their horses was easy, since Eclipse had not gone far, and Anne's horse had stayed with him. They found the 4 horses belonging to the shooters, and before allowing Lane to mount up, Clint searched all the saddlebags.

"Which one was Koenig's horse?" he asked.

"The roan," Lane said.

He spent more time on Koenig's saddlebags than the others, but still came up empty.

They mounted up and headed back to town, after Clint warned Lane that if he tried to escape, he would end up dead.

***

As they rode into town Clint looked around to see if anyone was paying special attention to them. He didn't notice anything but idle curiosity.

They went directly to the sheriff's office and dismounted.

"Inside, Lane," Clint said. "Anne, you want to go to your hotel?"

"I'm stickin' with you," she said.

Hoskins looked up from his desk and eyed them with curiosity.

"What's goin' on?" he asked.

"This feller and three others tried to ambush us outside of town," Clint said.

"And the other three?"

"Dead."

"Do we know who they were?"

"According to Lane here, they were named Harris, Beamish and Koenig."

"I know 'em all," Hoskins said, "includin' Lane, here. Don't you know better, boy?"

"It was a lot of money, Sheriff."

"Enough to risk gettin' killed?"

"Koenig said it wouldn't be hard," Lane complained.

"Well, I guess you saw how easy it really was," Hoskins said. He got up, grabbed his keys from a wall hook. "Get in a cell!"

He walked Lane into a cell, locked it and came back out.

"What do you know about these men?" Clint asked.

"Lane's an idiot," Hoskins said. "Beamish and Harris were troublemakers?"

"And Koenig?"

"I'm gonna tell you this, but I don't want you to go off half-cocked."

"I'm ready," Clint said.

"Koenig works—worked—security for Big Bill Bartlett at the Buffalo."

"That's the connection I was looking for."

"I said don't go off half-cocked."

"I'm not," Clint said. "I'll give Big Bill a chance to explain. Is the game still going on?"

"Still four players, last I heard," Hoskins said.

Clint knew games like that fell into periods where the chips simply moved around the table, from player to player, until somebody made a big move.

"Well," Clint said, "I guess we'll go over and have a look."

"See here, Adams," Hoskins said, "Big Bill is important to this town. Don't walk in there and start shootin'."

"Sheriff," Clint said, "I'm still looking for my man, Resnick. All I want from Big Bill is to know if he's hiding him."

"And," Anne added, "if Resnick paid Big Bill to have Clint killed."

"Now wait—"

"Relax, Sheriff," Clint said. "If I have anything to say about it, I've fired my last shot . . ."

"Good!"

". . . today."

"Adams!"

***

As Clint and Anne walked into the Buffalo Saloon, Clint immediately cast his eyes on Eddie, the bartender. He wanted to know if Eddie knew what his boss was up to. There didn't seem to be any surprise on the man's face, just a smile.

"Still four," Eddie said to Clint. "Nothin' much has happened since you left."

"So I heard from the sheriff. Two beers, Eddie."

"Comin' up."

He set the 2 mugs in front of them. Anne was looking over at the table, trying to see how many chips her husband had in front of him.

"His luck's been holdin', so far," Eddie told her.

She turned, said, "Thank you," and picked up her beer.

"Eddie, where's your boss?" Clint asked, picking his up, as well.

"I don't know," Eddie said. "Ain't seen him since you left."

"What about Koenig?"

"Ain't seen him today, either."

"That's because he's dead," Clint said.

"What?"

"He tried to ambush me and Anne this afternoon," Clint said. "I had to kill him."

"What the hell—why would he do that?"

"Because he and three other men were paid to do it," Clint answered.

"Three others? Who?"

Clint told him the names of the other men.

"I know them all," Eddie said. "What happ—are they all dead?"

"All but Lane."

"But why would Lane, a kid, do that?" Eddie asked, shaking his head. "It doesn't make sense."

"Maybe for the promise of a lot of money, it does," Anne answered.

"But money from who?" Eddie asked.

"That's what I want to ask your boss about. I understand Koenig worked here."

"That's right," Eddie said. "He was usually behind one of those walls."

Eddie pointed at the walls that had the gun turrets in them.

"And the others?"

"They drank here, but they didn't work here," Eddie said. "Beamish and Harris were usually looking for

179

trouble. Lane shouldn't have been around them. They were a bad influence on him."

"Obviously."

"Where is he now?" Eddie asked.

"In jail."

"Does he say who paid him?"

"He doesn't know," Clint said. "Koenig made the arrangements."

"This doesn't look very good for your boss, Eddie," Anne said.

"Now wait a minute," Eddie said. "Okay, so Koenig worked here, but hey, I work here, too. Does that mean I wanna kill you?"

"No," Clint said, "and that's why I'm not assuming anything. I asked your boss once, and I'm going to ask him again."

"Well," Eddie said, "he should be comin' back here. I don't see him missing the end of this tournament."

"Good point," Clint said. "We'll stay here and wait, and then we can all watch it together."

Chapter Forty-Three

"You're cheatin'!"

Big Bill hadn't returned yet. Clint and Anne were starting on their second beer each when Abel Terrell shouted from the table.

"That's a helluva accusation, Terrell," Luke Short said. "I've never known Bat Masterson to cheat in his life."

"Well, he's cheatin' now," Terrell said. "How else do you explain him beatin' me every hand."

"Maybe," Luke said, "he's just a better player than you."

Terrell jumped to his feet, knocking his chair over backwards.

"What's he doin'?" Anne said.

"He's losing," Clint said, "and he doesn't like it."

"Maybe I should—" Anne started to walk toward her husband, but Clint grabbed her arm.

"Don't," he said.

"But Bat'll kill him," she said.

"Not if he doesn't have to."

They continued to watch.

"Terrell," Bat said, looking up at the man, "in the old days if somebody accused me of cheatin' he'd be dead by now."

"Well, this ain't the old days," Terrell said. "I've been winning all week. Why would I start losing now?"

"Because now you're up against better players," Bat said.

"I'm the best player at this table!" Terrell insisted.

"You had the best luck," Luke said, "for a while. But now your luck has run out."

"Are you gonna call this hand," Bat asked, "or fold."

The 4th player at the table sat back and watched.

Terrell stared down at Bat's hand, 4 cards that he could see, and 3 that he couldn't. Luke was out of the hand, and watching, ready to use his gun.

"Well?" Bat asked.

"I call!" Terrell said, turning over his cards. "A flush."

Bat turned over his cards.

"Full house."

"You're out, Terrell," Luke said.

"Not a chance."

Anne could see her husband was going to go for his gun.

"Abel, don't!" she shouted.

But he was beyond listening. He was distraught at having lost and was going to react the only way he could. And either Bat, or Luke, or both would kill him.

She had to do something.

***

Clint also knew that Abel Terrell was about to make a fatal mistake. He could see that Anne was about to do something she probably would never be able to live with. So as she started to go for her gun he stopped her with his left hand, and drew his own gun. When he fired he sent a bullet into the back of Terrell's left thigh. The impact staggered him, and his leg folded beneath him and he fell to the floor.

Bat and Luke stood up and looked across the room at Clint.

Anne turned and looked at him, as well.

"I was going to—" she started.

"I know," Clint said. "I couldn't let you."

He walked across the room to where Terrell was lying on the floor, holding his hand to the back of his thigh. Ribbons of blood seeped between his fingers.

"What the hell—" he said, staring up at Clint. "You shot me?"

"Only to keep your wife from doing it," Clint said. "And, by the way, to keep you alive."

"Good job," Bat said. "He didn't look like he was going to leave me much choice."

"Let's get him out of here before he bleeds to death," Eddie suggested, coming around the bar. "He's out of the game, right?"

"Right," Luke said. "We're down to three."

"Well, Big Bill ain't here, so I figure you three should get back to your game while we take care of this," Eddie said, pointing down at Terrell.

"Right," Bat said.

"By the way," Clint said, pointing to the third player, "who's this?"

"Oh, you haven't met," Luke said. "Clint Adams meet Johnny Gambit."

Gambit stood up and extended his hand. Clint shook it.

"I've heard a lot about you," Gambit said.

"I've heard nothing about you," Clint said.

Gambit smiled.

"I kinda like it that way."

"Can we get this man to the doctor?" Eddie asked Clint.

"Yeah, yeah," Clint said.

"Joi!" Eddie shouted.

Clint hadn't seen Joi standing at the end of the bar, because she had been sitting in the back of the room, hidden from view. Now she appeared.

"I'll be right back," Eddie told her. "Keep an eye on things."

"I will," she said.

As Clint and Eddie picked Terrell up off the floor, Clint saw Joi pull Anne aside and whisper something to her. Then Anne hurried to go with them to the doctor's office.

"What was that about?" Clint asked.

"I'll tell you later," Anne promised.

Chapter Forty-Four

Clint, Eddie and Anne got Terrell to Doc Grady's, then headed back to the Buffalo to see the end of the tournament—if, indeed, it ended that evening.

Eddie was in a hurry and moved on ahead of them.

"What did Joi have to say?" Clint asked Anne.

"She said," Anne replied, "you might want to have a look behind the Buffalo."

"Behind it?"

"That's what she said."

"Well," Clint said, "I guess I might as well get that done now."

"It's gettin' dark," she said.

"I know," he said, "so I figure to do it before it gets darker. You can go back to the saloon. Or to the doctor's office and wait."

"Abel's not in the game anymore," she said. "I'll just stay with you, if you don't mind."

"Don't you want to make sure he's okay?"

"Clint," she said, "I was gonna shoot him myself, and I'm not sure it was gonna be in the thigh."

"Okay, then," Clint said, "let's go and have a look behind the Buffalo."

***

When they reached the Buffalo, Clint thought about going inside first, but then he figured Joi must have felt she was risking something, whispering to Anne like that. In the end he looked for an alley that would lead to the back, found it on one side of the building, and led Anne into it. Might as well take Joi's tip and pursue it.

"What could be back here?" Anne wondered.

"Maybe nothing," Clint said. "Maybe it's another ambush."

"Great." She put her hand on her gun.

"Relax," he said. "I don't think Joi would do that."

"Really?" she asked. "Are you and she . . . friends?"

"Not quite," he said.

They got to the back and saw a large empty lot spread out before them.

"An empty lot," Anne said.

The sun was down, but there was still some light before it was officially nightfall.

"Well," Clint said, "there is that."

She looked to where he was pointing.

"A shed?" she asked. "It looks like it'd fall down in a stiff wind."

"Well then," Clint said, "let's try not to breathe on it too hard."

***

Joi looked back at her boss' door, waiting for him to put in an appearance. He was going to want to watch the end of the game, but she also knew he had other things on his mind.

When Eddie came back, she got out from behind the bar and went back to her place at the far end, still looking around nervously.

She hoped the woman with Clint would tell him what she said about going behind the saloon. Big Bill had disappointed her when she sent her out there to "entertain" the man who was hiding there. She thought that he had more respect for her than that. Obviously she was wrong.

Maybe helping Clint Adams would help her get her respect back.

***

They crossed the empty lot toward the shed. When they reached it Clint turned and looked behind them. He could see the lights in the windows of the Buffalo, and knew anyone looking out one of those back windows would see them.

"Anne," he said, "keep an eye on the back of the building. Let me know if anyone comes out."

"I will."

"Or looks out a window."

"I'll try."

As Anne turned toward the back of the Buffalo, Clint moved closer to the shed's front door. There was no lock on it. He grasped the handle and pulled. The door opened on creaking hinges.

It was now almost fully dark, and he couldn't see inside. He dug into his pocket for a Lucifer match and struck it. In the flare of the flame he saw an oil lamp off to one side. As the match burned his finger it went out, so he grabbed the lamp, lit another match, and touched it to the lamp. The interior of the shed appeared in a yellow glow.

Now he knew he had to move fast. From the Buffalo anyone could see the light in the shed. Even if he closed the door, there were spaces between the wooden planks that formed the structure.

It looked like the place was simply used for storage. There were rags, and crates and tools, a tarpaulin toward the back.

"Anything?" Anne whispered.

"No . . . wait."

He looked down and noticed there were cigarette butts on the floor—a lot of them. Why would somebody stand in here and smoke? They wouldn't. But somebody who was staying here—maybe hiding out—would. He decided to look again. He moved some of the tools to look behind them, and beneath them, did the same with some of the crates. In the end there was only the tarp in the rear of the shed left. He carried the lamp there, held it high, grasped the edge and pulled it off of whatever it was covering.

A body.

"Anything?" Anne hissed again.

"Oh yeah!" he said.

She stuck her head in the door.

"What? Oh . . ."

He held the lamp closer to the body and turned the man over, onto his back.

"That's a big nose," she said.

"It sure is."

Chapter Forty-Five

Clint doused the lamp, left the shed and closed the door.

"Is that the man you've been trackin' for Roper?" she asked.

"That's him."

"Then your job is done," she commented.

"I suppose," he said. "My job was to find him and bring him back to Denver. But I'm not going to bring back his body. I'll just send Tal a telegram and let him know his man is dead."

"And then you're done," she said. "Because you already did what I wanted you to do."

"Which part?" he asked, thinking of being in bed with her.

"Well, that part, yes," she said, reading his mind. "But you also showed me that I'm right about my marriage. It's over."

"Are you sure?"

"Well," she said, "I was willing to shoot him myself before you did it."

"Yes," he said, "but to save his life."

"Well," she said, "I don't want him dead, I just want him gone."

"Let's get out of this lot."

They started back across to the Buffalo.

"So what now?" she asked. "You gonna head out tomorrow?"

"No," Clint said, "I still have to deal with this body."

"You said you'd send a telegram to Roper," she said. "What else?"

"I've got to tell the sheriff that I found him, where and how, and who I think killed him."

"Who?"

"Big Bill," Clint said. "I think he did it, or had it done."

"How was he killed?"

"His throat was cut."

"So if Resnick was paying Big Bill to have somebody get rid of you, why would he turn around and kill 'im?"

"Because the job wasn't getting done," Clint said. "And he had probably already been paid. He decided to get rid of him."

"How are you gonna prove that?"

"I'll lay it out for the sheriff and let him worry about it," Clint said.

"Do you think he'll pursue it?"

"To be honest, probably not."

"So Big Bill gets away with trying to have you killed, as well as killing a man."

"Well," Clint said, "when you put it that way . . ."

Chapter Forty-Six

Clint didn't bother going back to the Buffalo. He really wasn't concerned with who won the tournament. He figured it would either be Bat or Luke.

Instead, he went across to the Gold Rush and took Anne with him. The place was in full swing, but he simply intended to walk through on his way to his room. Since Anne was following, as he went by Lily, Bonnie and Darla, they all looked on curiously. Taft just watched with an amused grin.

When they got to his room Anne asked, "Those girls downstairs, friends of yours?"

"Sort of."

"I don't think they liked me comin' up here."

"I'm not worried about that," he said, unstrapping his gun. "Do you want to go to your own room?"

"No." She unstrapped her own gun. "I like it here just fine."

Once they had their guns off and hanging on opposite ends of the bedpost they went to work removing their own clothing, until they were both naked.

"Before we do anythin'," she said, "you need to know, I don't expect anythin' from you. Not beyond this night."

"There was a time," he said, "when I wouldn't have been happy to hear that, but it's past. I'm too set in my ways, Anne."

She laughed.

"I think I've known that even longer than you have," she told him.

They got onto the bed from opposite sides and met in the middle in a hot embrace that was only the beginning of a long night of good-bye . . .

***

As they dressed in the morning Clint asked, "What are you going to do?"

"Oh, I'll check on Abel, see how he's doin'," she said. "Make my peace with him. Then I'll just have to decide where to go from here."

Clint wished he had gotten a reply from one of his last telegrams. It would have helped her decide.

"What about you?"

"I'll go and talk to the sheriff now, see how he wants to handle the dead body in the shed."

"Do you think it'll still be there?"

"I hope so," Clint said. "Damn it, maybe I should've moved it. Crap! Well, if it isn't there then I can't prove anything."

"And Big Bill will get away with murder."

"And benefit from his poker tournament." Clint made a sour face. "It's going to be hard for me to leave with that being the outcome of all this."

"Then I hope the body's still there," she said.

Clint was ready first.

"You take your time here and do what you've got to do. Maybe we'll see each other again before we leave town."

"Maybe we will," she agreed. "If we don't, last night was . . . nice."

He could think of other words to describe the energetic night of lovemaking they had shared, but he said, "Yeah, it was."

***

Clint walked to the sheriff's office, found the man drinking coffee behind his desk.

"Have a cup," Hoskins said, "and tell me what's on your mind today?"

"A dead man," Clint said, pouring himself a cup from the pot on the stove. He sat and told Hoskins about the body in the shed.

"And it's your man?"

"It is."

Hoskins made a face.

"I know," Clint said, "Big Bill's a big man in this town."

"He's a little man with big influence," Hoskins said, "but I guess I'll have to prove to you—and others—that I can do my job." He stood up. "Come on, show me the body."

Chapter Forty-Seven

Clint led Sheriff Hoskins to the shed behind the Buffalo Saloon.

"Not locked," Hoskins said, when they reached the door.

"I guess Big Bill didn't lock Resnick in."

"But if there's a body in there, why not lock people out?" the lawman asked.

"Good question."

They opened the door, and the interior was bathed in sunlight. It took Clint seconds to realize that the body was gone.

"Damn it!" he swore. "I'm stupid. I should've moved it last night."

"Take it easy," Hoskins said, leaning over the tarpaulin that had been used to cover the body. "There's blood here—enough for me to believe you."

"So what next, then?" Clint asked.

"Let's go talk to Big Bill," Hoskins said. "Maybe we can shake him up a little."

As they walked back across the lot Hoskins asked, "Did you hear who won the poker game?"

"No," Clint said, "but I assumed it was Masterson or Short."

"Some fella named Johnny Gambit."

"Really?"

"Seems like Short and Masterson knocked each other out," Hoskins said. "At least, that's what I heard."

"Jesus. I didn't expect that."

They went back up the alley to the front of the Buffalo, where Hoskins pounded his fist on the locked front doors. They were opened by Joi. She was wearing a simple, cotton dress, nothing she would ever wear to work.

"Sheriff," she said, "Mr. Adams."

"We want to see Big Bill, Joi," Hoskins said.

"Well . . . come on in," she said, backing away.

They entered and she relocked the door.

"I'll see if the boss is awake."

As she went up the stairs, Eddie the bartender appeared from a doorway behind the bar.

"'mornin', gents," he said, slapping his hands down on the bar. "Coffee?"

"Yes, please," Clint said.

"I'll have a cup," the sheriff said.

Eddie poured two mugs and set them on the bar.

"What brings you here so early in the mornin'?" Eddie asked.

"A dead body," Hoskins said.

"Oh," Eddie said, "well, since I don't know nothin' about no dead bodies, why don't we talk about somethin' else?"

"What the hell happened in the game?" Clint asked. "How did Bat or Luke not win?"

"It came down to a big hand at the end," Eddie said, "and they played it like Gambit wasn't even there."

"But he was."

"Yep," Eddie said, "with aces and queens."

"Jesus!" Clint said. He couldn't believe his friends had underestimated another player so badly—and with his own favorite hand.

He hated coincidences!

At that moment Joi came back downstairs and approached the bar.

"The boss'll be down in a minute."

"Okay," Hoskins said.

"What's this about?" she asked.

"A dead body," Hoskins said, again. "In the shed in the back."

She shifted her gaze to Clint.

"You looked?"

"I did, last night."

"And was that your man?"

"It was."

"Then I'm sorry," she said.

"Why are you sorry?" Clint asked.

"Because I killed him."

She rubbed her upper arms, like she was cold.

"What?" Hoskins asked.

"Why?" Clint asked.

"Big Bill sent me back there to . . . entertain him," she said. "I didn't want to do it, but I went back there before I actually saw him. He was . . . ugly, and dirty, and mean." She hugged herself again, as if still chilled.

"So you killed him?" Hoskins asked.

"He wouldn't let me leave," she said. "I had to . . . convince him that I decided to stay and be nice to him. That's how I got behind him—"

"Never mind, Joi," Clint said, stopping her before she told the lawman that she had cut Resnick's throat. "Sounds like self-defense to me."

"Where's the body?" Hoskins asked.

"Big Bill moved it. I don't know where."

"Suits me," Clint said.

"What?" Hoskins asked.

"I'm satisfied," Clint said.

"Wait . . . your man is dead."

"Which means I found him," Clint said. "My job's done."

"And what about whoever tried to ambush you?" Hoskins asked, looking confused.

"Twice."

"Right, twice," Hoskins said.

"You've got Lane."

"He's a kid," Hoskins said. "He's not goin' to jail."

At that moment a door opened and closed upstairs and then Big Bill started down the stairs.

"Okay," Sheriff Hoskins said, "Then I'll just take him." He looked at Joi. "Will you testify that he sent men to ambush Clint Adams?"

"Yes," she said. "Big Bill does that, charges men to guarantee their safety, take care of whoever's after them."

"Why?" Hoskins asked. "Why does he do that when he has a successful place like the Buffalo?"

She shrugged.

"He likes it," she said. "It makes him feel . . . bigger."

"And will you also testify that he moved a dead body?"

"No," Clint said, waving his hand at Joi. "She'd have to say how she knew."

Hoskins turned to face Clint.

"You're not makin' it easy for me to do my job," he told him.

"Believe me, Sheriff," Clint said, "I'm just happy you're doing it."

Clint turned and Joi ran to unlock the door so he could walk out the front door.

The first shot was close. It missed Clint, but hit Joi right in the chest.

Chapter Forty-Eight

Clint didn't have to look for the shooter, this time. He was right in front of him.

It was Abel Terrell, limping across the street toward him.

"You shot me, you sonofabitch!" the man shouted.

He kept pulling the trigger on the gun he was holding. He was a terrible shot, his gun would be empty in seconds, but one bullet had found its way into Joi's chest, killing her. Clint just figured she deserved to be avenged, and at the same time he could save Anne Archer the cost of a divorce.

He drew and fired once, drilling Terrell right through the chest. The man staggered. His gun fell from his lifeless hand as he fell onto his face.

Hoskins came running out with his gun in hand, stopped when he saw the dead man.

"Know 'im?" he asked.

"Yeah," Clint said.

"Does he work for Big Bill?"

"Nothin' to do with that," Clint said. "This was just personal."

They both turned and looked down at Joi's body, lying half in, half out of the doorway.

"Where's Big Bill?" Clint asked.

"Inside," Hoskins said. "Eddie's keepin' an eye on him."

"Eddie?"

"He's a law-abidin' citizen," Hoskins said. "Big Bill ain't goin' nowhere."

"You don't have Joi's testimony, anymore," Clint said.

"I'll try doin' without it," Hoskins said. "Meanwhile, I'll have these bodies moved, and put him in a cell next to Lane."

"I appreciate that, Sheriff," Clint said.

"Just doin' my job, Adams," Hoskins said, "just doin' my job."

***

The bodies had been removed, Big Bill was in a cell, and Eddie the bartender was keeping the Buffalo open for business. Life goes on, Clint thought, and that was when he saw the rider coming up the street.

He had gone to Anne Archer's hotel to tell her what happened to her husband. She listened to him, said, "He left you no choice," and closed her door. At that point Clint thought he would never see her again.

But he had sent two telegrams out, and this was the response to one of them. He hoped it would do a lot to raise her spirits. She didn't have to love her husband to be sad he was dead.

He stepped out so that the rider would see him and stop.

"I thought you'd send a telegram," he said.

"I decided to just come," the rider said. "Where is she?"

"I think at her hotel," Clint said. "Follow me."

He headed for Anne Archer's hotel, with the rider close behind. He hoped she would be there, and they wouldn't have to go looking for her.

When they reached the hotel he said, "Wait down here. She'll be surprised."

"Can I wait in a saloon? I'd like to have a beer."

"Sure," he said. "I'll bring her to the Gold Rush, down the street."

The rider nodded and rode that way.

***

Clint knocked on the door, hoping she would be there. When she opened it he was pleased, and she was surprised.

"I didn't expect to see you again," she said. "This is a nice surprise."

"I have a better one for you," he said. "Come with me."

"Wait." She walked to the bed, took her gun belt from the post and strapped it on. "Might as well get used to this again." She stepped into the hall and asked, "Where are we goin'?"

"The Gold Rush," he said. "I'm going to buy you a beer."

"That's my surprise?"

"You'll see."

***

All the while Clint walked Anne over to the Gold Rush she was quiet, not asking any questions. But when they walked in she took one look at the woman who was standing at the bar—all the men in the place looking at her, as well—and almost screamed.

"Sandy!"

Her old partner, Sandy Spillane, hurried over to her and the 2 women embraced—to the pleasure of the men present.

"Why don't we go outside?" Clint suggested.

The women remained arm-in-arm as they went back out the batwing doors.

"What—how—why are you here?" Anne stammered.

"Clint hunted me down and sent me a telegram," Sandy said.

Clint had met Anne Archer, Sandy Spillane, and Katy Littlefeather at the same time, when they were all hunting bounties together.

"You did this?" Anne asked.

"I thought it might cheer you up."

"Omigod!" she said. "She hugged him, then hugged the blonde Sandy again. Clint noticed that Spillane had aged, but they all had. She was still a handsome specimen of a woman, dressed for the trail with a gun on her hip.

"Still a bounty hunter, Sandy?" Clint asked.

"Never stopped," Sandy said, "but I miss my partners."

"Do you miss me enough to let me come back?" Anne asked.

"Of course!"

"And where's Katy?" Anne asked.

"I don't know that, Anne," Sandy said, "but why don't we go and find her. I mean, that's what we do, ain't it?"

Anne looked at Clint, who said, "That sounds like a great idea to me."

Coming November 27, 2018

THE GUNSMITH
442
The Last Wagon Train

For more information
visit: www.speakingvolumes.us

On Sale Now!

THE GUNSMITH
440
Lost Man

**For more information
visit:** www.speakingvolumes.us

On Sale Now!

THE GUNSMITH
438

For more information
visit: www.speakingvolumes.us

On Sale Now!

THE GUNSMITH
436

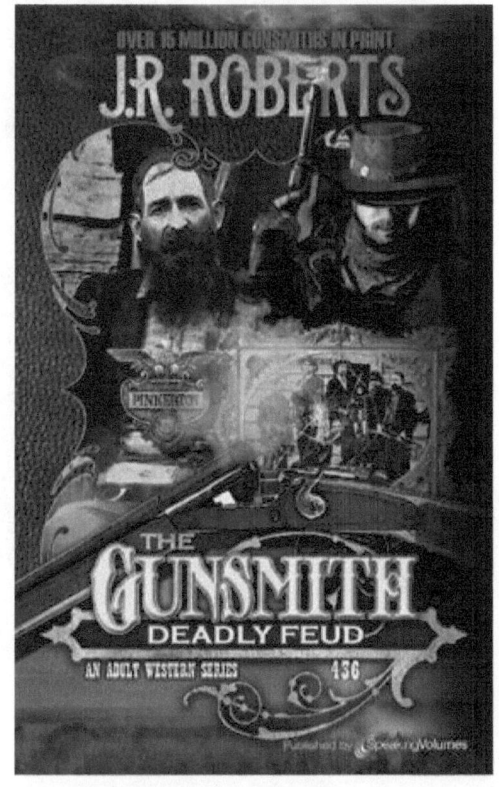

For more information
visit: www.speakingvolumes.us

On Sale Now!

THE GUNSMITH
434

For more information
visit: www.speakingvolumes.us

On Sale Now!

THE GUNSMITH
433

For more information
visit: www.speakingvolumes.us

On Sale Now!

THE GUNSMITH
431

For more information
visit: www.speakingvolumes.us

On Sale Now!

THE GUNSMITH
430

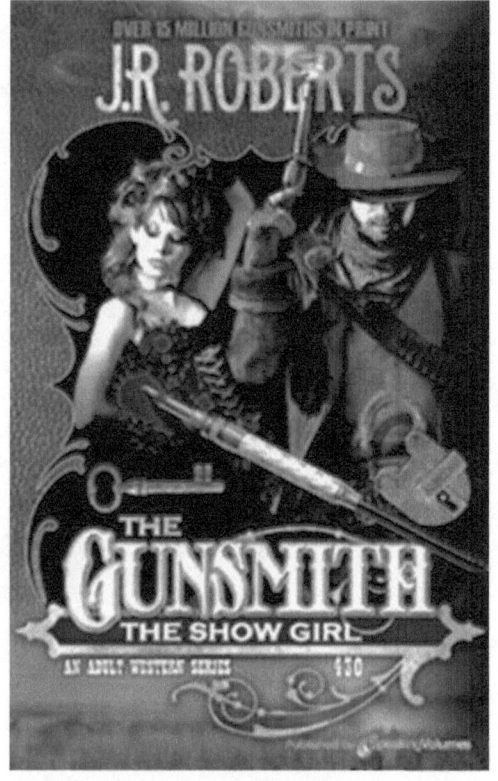

For more information
visit:

On Sale Now!

TRACKER *series*
by
Award-Winning Author
Robert J. Randisi (J.R. Roberts)

On Sale Now!

MOUNTAIN JACK PIKE *series*
by
Award-Winning Author
Robert J. Randisi (J.R. Roberts)

For more information
visit: www.speakingvolumes.us

www.ingramcontent.com/pod-product-compliance
Lightning Source LLC
Chambersburg PA
CBHW032044240626
47154CB00003B/1069